TEACH YOURSELF TREACHERY

Rachel Petersen's husband had drowned in Holland — so who is the man who appears at her house and claims to be that husband, substantiating his claim with a passport and detailed recollections of their brief married life? From the moment the stranger calling himself Erik Flemming Petersen steps through the door, there is no peace for Rachel. She determines to unravel the tangled threads of the mystery — only to find they are more tightly woven than she could have suspected . . .

JOHN BURKE

TEACH YOURSELF TREACHERY

Complete and Unabridged

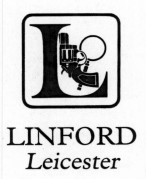

LINFORD
Leicester

First published in Great Britain

First Linford Edition
published 2013

A catalogue record for this book is available
from the British Library.

ISBN 978–1–4448–1725–6

Published by
F. A. Thorpe (Publishing)
Anstey, Leicestershire

Set by Words & Graphics Ltd.
Anstey, Leicestershire
Printed and bound in Great Britain by
T. J. International Ltd., Padstow, Cornwall

This book is printed on acid-free paper

1

The two widows, the old and the young, sat on the rostrum beneath the monument. There were four men with them, one on his feet, talking. Behind lay the muddy floor of the reclaimed polder. Before them the waves bit and snarled at the outer wall of the dike, thwarted now but denying a lasting defeat. The monument rose into the steely sky like an admonitory finger, warning the sea to advance no further.

Today the autumn wind threatened winter. The people clustering below the rostrum put their hands in their pockets and blinked up sideways at the man who was trying to make himself heard. His words were snatched from his mouth and blown away across the flat expanse that would one day be fields and farms and towns. Here the world was divided into two grey sections, distinguished from each other only by the great curve of the new wall. On one side the sea rolled away to the horizon; on the other, the waves of mud and the trapped pools faded into a distance edged faintly with the far-enclosing arm of the dike. Only the memorial column and, two miles away along the dike, the church tower of Stevinstad made vertical protest above the low land and the vast plain of the sea.

The Dutch phrases rolled thickly out from the man on the rostrum, and the wind swallowed them up.

Rachel Petersen leaned back and glanced behind him at her grandmother. Old Mrs Watson did not appear to feel the cold. She did not seem to be aware of anybody or anything. With her head sagging, her eyes fixed on the planks of the temporary platform, she must be thinking of things remote in space and time. Or else she was just not thinking at all: sunk deep in her old, vague resentments, she no longer heard any sound from the surface.

Surely, thought Rachel, the man must soon finish his speech. She knew little Dutch, in spite of the time she had spent here, but she could not believe that all those words were necessary. The dike had been sealed, the road encircled the polder, the memorial was now another proud, secure landmark on the coast of Holland. What more was there to say? Promises of new land in the future, congratulations on achievement, a few conventional remarks about this land of fishermen and farmers: the usual patriotic thunder. Only it was a thunder muted by the unchecked wind and the insistent mutter of the water against the wall.

There was a burst of applause. And then, heavily and portentously, the speaker was stumbling into English. He turned towards Mrs Watson and bowed; turned away from her towards Rachel and bowed again.

He said: 'It is sad but proud for us to have our two distinguished guests with us. These two ladies mean much to us. Professor Watson did much for us. Much. Our museum, the great things of our past . . . he worked with us as a friend, and we cannot repay. We cannot ever repay. And Mr Petersen, who was here such a short time.'

Was there a respectful murmur of sympathy or was it the wind lowering its voice derisively for a moment?

'It was a privilege to us to have one of the world's greatest scholars . . . experts . . . a man whose knowledge of Viking history taught us new things in our own history. When we drained the sea-bed Professor Watson was with us. When we won new land he showed us the meaning of the old land. Our heritage . . . '

Rachel turned her head away. It must look as though she were ignoring the speaker, but in fact it was the only way she could hear clearly.

Mrs Watson did not move. Her head was still bowed as though in acknowledgment of the reference to her husband. But it was doubtful whether she had heard. It was doubtful whether she wanted to hear.

Perhaps, thought Rachel, the old lady ought never to have been brought over from England for this ceremony. The ceremony meant nothing to her; the sentiments their hosts expressed about her late husband meant nothing to her.

'We think of them,' the voice went on,

4

'as true friends of our country. They lost their lives here searching for . . . for truths . . . about our past. We wish they were here with us today, when we meet to open — to unveil — our monument, here where the wall was finally closed.'

Rachel turned to look out to sea, and at once the words were engulfed.

She, too, wished her grandfather could have been here today. He would have enjoyed every minute of it, even if the wind had risen to a howling gale. He liked to be praised. He liked to be told he was a great man and a benefactor. There had been, goodness knows, plenty of stuffy old enemies to tell him the opposite. He liked to be called Professor, though he would earnestly and honestly protest that he was not entitled to this. Not entitled to it academically; but how he had hated the academics, and how they had hated him! He deserved to have been here today. He had devoted years to this place, and he should have been here for the solemnity of it all and the ritual hand-shaking that would go on afterwards.

But the water that had been beaten

back so that he could reclaim so many treasures had, in the end, claimed him. He and Erik were dead now — he washed back with the fragments of the shattered boat, so that he might be the first to be buried, with great honour, in the new churchyard of Stevinstad; and Erik . . . Where was Erik? Swept away, where would his body come to rest? Perhaps it would be found some day by a Hammond Watson of the future, turning over the mud and unearthing ship's timbers, pottery, weapons, and bones. The bones of Erik Petersen . . .

Rachel knew that she ought to feel horror, or at the very least the hollow, echoing sadness of loss. But when she thought of their brief marriage, and knew that she would not see Erik again, she was conscious only of a shameful relief. Two months since he had gone, and she admitted to it — to relief. She tried to push it swiftly out of her mind, but no other word would do.

There was a shuffle of feet. The ceremony was over. The six on the rostrum stood up, and somebody was shaking Mrs Watson's hand. Mrs Watson pushed herself up out of her chair, looking blank.

Rachel edged along the platform towards her.

'All over, Grandma.'

The old lady grunted. 'It took long enough. Now where is a fire? Where is something warm to drink?'

Adrian was waiting attentively at the foot of the three steps. He put up his hand under Mrs Watson's elbow to guide her down. She grunted again, almost derisively, and slithered past him. Adrian smiled up at Rachel.

Rachel said: 'Could you hear anything down there?'

'Not a word. Did he say anything very compelling?'

'I couldn't answer for the Dutch part. There was a bit about Grandad in English, on nice routine lines.'

She lowered her voice on the last few words, not to offend the people who were closing in on them. There were men who had worked with her grandfather, and a cluster of dignitaries from towns beyond the polder. There was a man from The Hague who had never met Hammond Watson but wanted to shake hands with someone to show how much he appreciated something or other. And there were a couple of plump women who intended to make the most of this historic occasion.

Adrian managed to break the onward surge. It was hard to tell precisely how he did it, but Rachel was once more conscious of her gratitude towards him. She could not have managed without him these last few weeks. Or, at any rate, not managed so well. He had taken a great deal of strain and irritation from her. Adrian had not merely made it his business to sort out the problems that had arisen in the settling of her grandfather's estate: he had a soothing competence in turning the most everyday things to the best advantage. Things had a habit of going the way he wanted them to, simply because he took it as his right that they should do so. Now, by some faintly aggressive curl of the lip, he was making it clear that people ought to know better than to crowd in on the two widows.

There were a few perfunctory handshakes and then he was guiding them towards the car.

Rachel glanced covertly at his face, sharp-edged against the sweep of the sky.

Adrian Brent was taller than she. Not as tall as her husband had been; but, then, she would not have wanted anyone ever again as Danish and savage and overpowering as Erik. Adrian's strength was in his very quietness, his almost contemptuous reserve. You saw it in his dark face, with the restrained smile that rarely broke into a laugh, and the brown eyes that were steady and yet so often secretive and withdrawn.

He was, she thought — seeing him against the background of fair, red-cheeked Dutchmen — very English. His family, although going through difficult times, had managed to send him to his father's old school; and family and school and country had made him what he was.

'If this wind gets any worse,' he said, sliding in behind the wheel of the car, 'we'll get blown off the dike into the mud.'

9

They were buffeted all the two miles back to Stevinstad. It was a jarring, thumping sensation that stopped only when they turned off the sea road into the only other street that the little town so far possessed.

In years to come this would be a town of ten thousand inhabitants. As the polder, that tract of saturated land within the containing wall, was being drained, cleared by reeds, trenched, and gradually converted into agricultural land, the houses would multiply. The plan was already laid down, just as the plan for the polder was laid down: sections would be methodically developed, families would move in as methodically as the seeds dropped into the ground. But today there were only three hundred here. Most of them were engineers and workmen — the men who had built the wall. There was already a church. The houses were trim and red, with bright doors and wide, white-rimmed windows. There was one shop so far, and a café.

And there was the museum.

The car swung in beside the long, low building. The monument they had just left, two miles away, was a memorial to the achievement of those men who had wrested yet another tract of land from the sea. Within the walls of the museum was Hammond Watson's personal memorial — his collection of treasures drawn from the slimy bed of that conquered sea.

Beside it was Hammond Watson's house. It was probably the only example in this country of priority being given to the house of a foreign archaeologist rather than to homes for the people who would work on the land.

A man came out of the museum as Adrian held the car door open for Rachel. Getting out, she stepped away from the car while Adrian helped her grandmother stiffly out.

The stranger stared keenly at her, then came quickly forward.

'You would be Mrs Petersen?'

He was American, in his middle forties, with a sallow face and oddly pale, disillusioned eyes.

Adrian, still occupied with old Mrs Watson, frowned discouragingly over his shoulder.

Rachel said: 'I am.'

'You must be mighty proud of the work your grandfather did.'

'Naturally.'

'I was going to go along to the ceremony — looks like the whole town was there — but I couldn't tear myself away from that collection. And I hear there's plenty more. He left it all to you, isn't that right?'

'A lot of it,' said Rachel coolly, 'wasn't his to leave. It belongs to various institutions who subsidized his work.'

'Sure, sure. But he was allowed to keep quite a bit, so they say. And I reckon you know it all, anyway. I mean, if there was a chance of getting to see the things that haven't been put on show to the public — '

'We are very busy sorting things out,' said Rachel. 'Cataloguing and so on.'

'I'd esteem it a great privilege some-time if — '

'The ladies are very tired.' Adrian was at Rachel's shoulder now, his arm supporting Mrs Watson. 'It's been a very full day, and this isn't really a suitable time for discussing Mr Watson's collection.'

He shepherded the two of them down the path and into the house. Turning in through the door, Rachel saw from the corner of her eye that the American was standing watching them. She was half-surprised that he didn't whip out a camera and catch them for ever in a photograph. He simply stared. Out of reverence for the man they had known?

The presence of her grandfather seemed very real.

It was even more real and immediate inside the house. She had spent so much time and done so much work here with him. It was still impossible, after two months, to believe that he would not come out of his study flourishing some new chart that the Rijkswaterstaat had sent him and announcing that he was going to concentrate on this corner or that.

'I suppose the girl's not back from the ceremony yet,' said Adrian. 'I'd better go and make coffee for us.'

'I'll do it,' said Rachel.

He put his hand soothingly on her arm. 'Sit back and relax. You and Mrs Watson.'

He went briskly out of the room. Rachel heard the kitchen door open and swing shut again.

The sitting-room was quiet. Mrs Watson huddled in the armchair that had always been her husband's, though she was unaware of this: she had never been here before. While Hammond Watson scoured the coasts of Europe in his researches into Viking history she had sat at home in England. Or had she ever regarded England as home? Now, as she sat there muttering to herself she sounded alien. It was impossible to tell what she was muttering about or in what language. Sometimes scraps of her old Danish tongue came back in conversation, and perhaps that was what she was mouthing now; but, as she blurred over everything anyway, it made little difference.

Rachel had never been able to conjure up any picture of her grandmother as a young woman. There were two framed photographs yellowing on the wall back in Northumberland, but they conveyed nothing. The expressionless face revealed nothing — no sign of life or character, and somehow no marked physical traits, beautiful or otherwise.

It was inevitable that Hammond Watson, with his passion for Scandinavian history, should have married a girl from the North. But had she perhaps been a disappointment: had she ever been the fair, magnificent Viking that one would have liked to envisage? In the five years during which Rachel had lived with them, since the death of her mother and father in a plane smash, the two of them had seemed complete strangers to each other. They shared nothing; one felt that they had never shared anything. The great man went his own blustering, exuberant way while his wife shrivelled into a crone, shut away in that dank house near the North Sea. She was like a dark spirit out of Danish mythology rather than a living human being.

Suddenly Rachel realized that her grandmother had lifted her head and was looking around. This clean, bright, modern house was as different from the one in Northumberland as any house could be. And the eyes, suddenly bright, were perhaps making a bitter assessment. Here was where her famous husband had spent his time. Not with her, but with relics of the distant past of her people and of the Dutch. Relics in a sparkling new house, and relics in a bright new museum. Relics that for him were more alive, it seemed, than she had ever been. The house and its surroundings were hostile to her.

Rachel said: 'Adrian's making some coffee, Grandma. He won't be long.'

Mrs Watson's gaze came round to her, sharp and disconcerting. 'Oh,' she said. And then she said: '*Him* . . .'

Rachel checked a brusque question. It was no good demanding why her grandmother should speak in that tone of voice. There was not necessarily any reason in it at all. A question would probably meet with dour silence. Better to leave it alone.

But Mrs Watson went on: 'Your grandfather never liked him. You know that.'

'He's done a lot for us these last few weeks,' said Rachel. 'I don't know how we'd have cleared up everything without him.'

'He always wanted to meddle. Wanted to get his hands on things. Your grandfather,' she repeated, 'never liked him.'

'If he'd known him better — '

'He didn't want to know him any better.'

'You're very ungrateful, Grandma, after all he's done for us.'

Mrs Watson said: 'Are you going to marry him?'

Rachel felt herself flushing absurdly. 'What a fantastic idea! I've no thought whatever of marrying again. Not for a long time, anyway. It hasn't occurred to either of us — Adrian or myself.'

'It's occurred to *him*,' said the old lady stubbornly.

'Really, Grandma . . . '

'It occurred to him,' Mrs Watson went on, 'before you met Erik Petersen. And now he thinks of it again. I can see it. He wanted to get into the family then, and now it is on his mind once more.'

And what, Rachel was on the verge of asking, was so very wrong with that? But she restrained herself. It was no good tilting against the old lady's prejudices.

She wondered how true it was that Adrian wanted to marry her. She wanted to think about it, and yet at the same time she wanted to keep all such speculations out of her head. Really, she had behaved badly to Adrian. There had certainly been a time when he had seemed to be moving towards her, and she had been waiting for him to speak. But he had not spoken: he had left it too late. He had not been sure enough — perhaps of her, perhaps of himself; he had been quiet and attentive and likeable, and it had not been enough. Erik had appeared and swept her off her feet.

Now Adrian was with her again, and she had the same awareness of his nearness. This time she was not impatient. His quiet concern for her was what she needed. Later — perhaps not all that much later — there would be time for plans and a new life.

She said: 'He's been a good friend to us, Grandma, and that's all there is to it. When you think of the unfinished work in the museum that he tidied up, and the details he smoothed over for us . . . He's the one who's made it possible for us to leave everything just the way it ought to be for the people who'll be taking over. We're lucky to have had an expert — '

'Your grandfather,' mused Mrs Watson, 'always hated experts. And,' she added, 'he particularly disliked young men who wanted to hang on to his coat-tails.'

One would have thought that she had abruptly decided to remember her husband with affection, as though he had always made a practice of confiding his views in her. But in another five minutes or so these flickers of uncertain memory would die down and she would be lost once more in her own twilight world.

The doorbell rang. Rachel got up from her chair, but Adrian called out: 'All right. Leave it to me.'

She turned in the middle of the room. The bronze shield on the wall cast back a burnished, distorted picture of her face.

In this mirror her hazel eyes were unnaturally wide, and as she moved forward her lips slid across the uneven surface in what might have been a wild grin or a rictus of fear. She was glad to meet her own true reflection in the mirror set close to the window — what she thought of as her very ordinary face, trim and uncomplicated, with its pugnacious little nose, small chin, and the auburn crown of hair that was the only possible echo of the shield, with its gloss of hinted bronze.

'Some hanger-on, I suppose,' said Mrs Watson distantly. 'Or another of those awful disciples. All the same.'

Rachel heard the buzz of voices. Adrian's seemed to rise in incredulity, then was silent. His footsteps came back from the front door, and he appeared in the room. His face was white. He stared at her, as incredulous as he had sounded — and almost, she thought, accusing.

'Someone to see you, Rachel.' It was little more than a whisper.

'But why do I have to see anybody? Couldn't you send them away? We've gone through the motions. We've been to the unveiling, we've let ourselves be photographed and gaped at. I don't want to see anybody.'

'I think you'd better.'

She had never seen Adrian look like this. For once his self-confidence had been sapped. Rachel said: 'What's wrong?'

'Will you come out . . . to the door . . . into the study, that is . . . for a moment?'

Her grandmother had sunk back into a reverie. That was the easiest way of avoiding conversation or unwelcome visitors. You simply withdrew into yourself. Rachel was too young for this. She followed Adrian out into the hall. He nodded towards the study at the front of the house, overlooking the sea road.

'In there.'

'What's the matter — who is it?'

Adrian said, with difficulty: 'It's your husband.'

Rachel tried to speak. No words would come. Automatically her feet carried her past Adrian, as though her body had the power to force her towards Erik when her

21

mind rebelled against him.

She went into the study.

Against the harsh grey sea-light through the window was the tall shape she remembered, the shoulders as broad as she remembered them, the whole outline just as she remembered, so unwillingly. The light lay on his flaxen, almost bleached hair.

Rachel moved to one side so that the sullen glare was no longer behind him. She forced herself to speak.

'Erik . . . '

Now she could see him full-face. He was smiling, with a strange mockery on his lips.

She had never seen him before in her life.

2

'You said you were my husband,' gasped Rachel.

He shook his head. It was a barbaric head, proud and aggressive under its helmet of fair hair; yet the man's strength was somehow not barbaric and primitive. He was like Erik yet unlike him. He had a family likeness to Erik, but it was not the likeness of a brother: he was simply a member, she thought, of the Danish family. There was a frightening vitality in his features. They were not the sunken, unilluminated features of the men you saw in London streets, on trains, in hotels. You were at once struck, almost physically, by the intensity of the man, with its threat of underlying violence.

Now he said smoothly: 'Those were not exactly my words.' His voice had the faintest lilt, the Danish inflection that was so like Welsh. 'Your friend did not deliver my message as I gave it.'

'I was told — '

'I said I was Erik Petersen.' He was still smiling. 'But, then, that is the same thing, is it not?'

Erik had been wild, impulsive . . . vicious. This man had a maturity that Erik could never have attained. In his face was an all-knowing amusement that was immediately disturbing.

'How dare you come in here and pretend — '

'Not a very nice welcome, Rachel. You are not glad to see me alive?'

'I don't know if you think this is a joke,' said Rachel unsteadily. 'If so, it's one in very poor taste. Perhaps you'll be good enough to go.'

'But we belong together.'

He took a step towards her. Rachel stumbled backwards, and at once Adrian was in the room. He must have been standing immediately outside the door, waiting to intervene.

Rachel lurched towards him. He put his arm round her shoulders. She was still so bewildered by the stranger that she only half-realized that this was the first time Adrian had touched her in this way.

'Adrian — this man says he's my husband.'

'And isn't he?'

'Certainly not.'

Adrian's hand squeezed her shoulder reassuringly. His arm slid away, he frowned that frown of his, and then he was advancing on the newcomer.

'What the blazes is the game?'

'You try to step into my shoes,' said the man gently, 'so soon?'

'Mrs Petersen says you claim to be her husband. Her husband, Erik Petersen, is dead.'

'But I am Erik Petersen, and I am not dead.'

Rachel said: 'It's a common enough name. There must be hundreds of Erik Petersens in Denmark.'

'Not so many on Hennesø,' he said.

She stared, again struck speechless. Hennesø had been Erik's home — a small island in the Kattegat to which she had never been because he would not have any contact with his parents.

'On Hennesø,' the incredible intruder

repeated. 'At Hvidfelt. Right?'

'You knew him,' Rachel burst out. 'All right, you knew him, you knew where he lived. But it's . . . it's cruel of you to come here talking like this. It's not a joke. I don't understand it.'

Adrian said: 'Get out before I throw you out.'

The tall fair man nodded down tolerantly at Adrian, but made no other move.

'I wish my dear wife would not persist in calling me cruel,' he said.

'I haven't noticed her using the word more than once,' said Adrian curtly.

'You were not there before. Three days after we were married — you remember, Rachel?'

A cold shiver ran through her. She remembered all right; but how could *he* speak confidently like that when he had not been with her? When nobody had been with her but Erik; Erik and herself together; Erik snarling at her and arousing in her a terror that she had never known. Why had he hated her so much? How could he have married her and then . . . ?

She snatched her mind away from that memory. It was hideous enough in itself. How could any other human being know of that hideousness?

'And,' she heard him saying, as though in a dream, 'there was the time when we went out along the wall. A windy day, I believe it was. When I talked of my ancestors and what they did to the women of England when they got at them.' He was watching her unwaveringly. He might have been jabbing experimentally at her, trying to make her wince. And yet it *was* only experimental — not savage, as Erik's attacks had been. 'You never called your grandfather cruel because of his interest in our history, but you called me cruel.'

'It was the way you . . . he . . . said it,' Rachel faltered. 'But it wasn't you. It wasn't!'

'How do I come to have these memories, then? Are you so anxious to get rid of me, Rachel, that you will pretend not to remember?'

Rachel was aware of Adrian's uneasiness. He had glanced at her once, and now was staring up at the man who called himself Erik Petersen.

She said: 'I'll go and telephone the police.'

Adrian started. 'You don't have to. I said I'd throw him out, and I will.'

There was no fear in him. He was quite prepared to tackle the bigger man. But Rachel caught his arm.

'No. That wouldn't help. He's mad. If you threw him out he might come back. Just keep an eye on him while I telephone the police.'

The man laughed. 'The police are a long way away along the dike,' he pointed out. 'Stevinstad does not need police yet. It is too small and too quiet. Charming, I think.'

Rachel turned on her heel and went towards the door.

'Rachel.' He used her name casually, as though he had been accustomed to do so. In fact, it seemed to come out more readily than it had ever come from Erik. Rachel tried not to stop, but he was calling her back. 'You ought to see this first. The police will think you are telling them a very odd story when I show them this.'

She stopped. There was a silence. Turning, she saw that he was already showing something to Adrian. Adrian stood very still. When he raised his eyes it was to stare in bewilderment at Rachel.

She felt herself being drawn back into the room.

Adrian said awkwardly: 'Rachel, you're quite sure . . . ?'

'You mean' — unhappy laughter bubbled in her throat — 'you think I don't even know who my own husband was?'

The Dane was holding out something to her. It was his passport. It said that his name was Erik Flemming Petersen, that he had been born on 28th May 1929, and that his place of residence was Hvidfelt, Hennesø. That all fitted. Rachel's fingers trembled. She wanted to snatch the passport from him and tear it, drag away at it until it was in fragments. But that would not destroy this man. He would still be here, still mocking her with his fantastic claim.

Adrian ventured: 'If you're quite sure — '

'Of course I'm quite sure. Adrian, can't you see that this is some sort of monstrous hoax?'

As though accepting this as a challenge, the Dane took two envelopes from his pocket. They were addressed to Erik Petersen at Hvidfelt.

'These don't prove anything,' cried Rachel wildly. 'You could have got them from anywhere.'

'Oh, come now, Rachel,' protested Adrian. 'The only person he could have got them from . . .'

His voice faded into a whisper. Rachel knew that he must have had the same idea as she had just had. It sprang to both their minds.

She said: 'That's it! You got them from Erik. You . . . you found the body. Where is it? Where was it washed up?'

'These documents,' said the man smoothly, 'have not been soaked in water. I think that is clear, yes?'

It was true enough.

'But where did you get them?' Rachel tried to keep a note of hysteria under control, not to let it rise too wildly high.

He said: 'It is easy. I am Erik Petersen of Hvidfelt, and I married you in the . . . the *borgerlig vielse* . . . you called it a registry office, I remember . . . the office in Vesterbro. It is so simple. Why do you make it so difficult, Rachel?'

'Get out!' The scream burst from her. She could no longer keep it down. This was a grotesque nightmare, and perhaps if she screamed hard enough she would be able to wake herself up. 'Get out — go away, and play your cheap tricks on someone else.'

Behind her, her grandmother said querulously: 'What is all the fuss about? I could hear you arguing from the sitting-room.'

Adrian slipped past Rachel and tried to take Mrs Watson's arm. 'Do come back and sit down, Mrs Watson. I'm sorry you've been kept waiting for your coffee. We got discussing something, and I'm afraid I haven't been keeping an eye on it.'

The old lady jerked herself away from him.

'Why were you screaming, Rachel?' she

demanded. 'And who is this visitor?'

'He says he's Erik Petersen,' said Rachel shakily.

'Oh.' Mrs Watson looked up at the intruder with eyes suddenly as blue as his own. 'So you are alive, then?'

'Yes.'

'You kept your wife waiting a long time before letting her know.'

'That is true,' he said apologetically.

Mrs Watson continued to gaze at him. He met her gaze levelly. Abruptly she said: 'I remember your mother. You're very like her.'

Rachel tensed. And so, she saw, did the man.

'But, Grandma,' Rachel fumbled, 'that's ridiculous. I don't know this man. He's not my husband.'

'You told me you had married Erik Petersen from Hennesø.'

'Yes, but — '

'This is Erik Petersen from Hennesø,' said the old lady firmly. 'I know his nose. And his mother's upper lip.' She chuckled. 'There was a lot of laughter in Tove.'

'There was,' he said, 'and is.'

'And your aunt Margrethe?'

'She was my great-aunt,' he said softly.

Mrs Watson stiffened. Then she nodded. 'Yes. Yes, so she was.' Her head went on nodding. 'She went to live in Langeland.'

'She died there just after the war.'

'Did she? Yes' — the head nodded confirmation once more — 'I believe somebody wrote and told me.'

Rachel said desperately: 'Grandma — you must listen. This man is not my husband. I've never seen him before. Never.'

'I cannot stand here for ever,' said Mrs Watson. 'We will go into the sitting-room.'

The Dane was at once beside her, gravely guiding her out of the room and across to the sitting-room door. He towered over her, seeming huge and yet being very gentle and respectful with the old lady.

The nightmare would not collapse. Rachel could not break the spell.

Adrian caught her up as she began to move forward.

'Rachel,' he murmured. 'You're quite sure about all this?'

'You don't believe me,' she said

passionately. 'You really think he's my husband, don't you?'

'He sounds so plausible.'

'But he isn't. I know. Adrian, I *know*. If you don't back me up . . . if I'm left on my own . . . '

'I'll back you up,' he said. But to Rachel he still sounded doubtful.

She said: 'While I go in with him and Grandma, won't you ring the police? It's the only way to put an end to this awful farce.'

'But what can the police do? His papers seem to be in order.'

'They're not *his* papers. He's a fraud. He must have found Erik's body — or . . . or murdered him, even.'

'But why?'

'There must be some way of proving that he's an impostor. Adrian — if he *were* Erik . . . which he's not, I swear he's not . . . would he have waited so long before coming back? And why has he shown up now? What does it all mean?'

From the sitting-room they heard the murmur of voices. Mrs Watson was talking more animatedly than Rachel had heard her talk for a long time.

Adrian said: 'If he came here and worked — er, your real husband, I mean — there ought to be plenty of people in Stevinstad who remember him.'

'Of course,' said Rachel. And then she said: 'Well . . . '

'Well,' Adrian insisted; 'aren't there?'

'He was here for only a few days before the accident. There must have been some of the workmen who met him with my grandfather, but I wouldn't know which ones.'

'We can find out.'

'They may not remember him terribly well. He wasn't unlike this man. And they wouldn't have seen much of him. Erik and Grandad went off together almost at once. My grandfather took to him, and he didn't often do that. They went off on one of Grandad's scavenging expeditions, and Grandad would have avoided people as far as possible. He was awkward, you know.'

'Yes, I know,' remembered Adrian ruefully.

There was the click of a door at the

back of the house, and a moment later their girl, Anne-Marie, appeared. She was a plump little local girl, flushed now with apologies for her lateness. Adrian explained about the coffee, and asked her to bring three cups into the sitting-room.

The two voices continued to rise and fall, and Anne-Marie glanced doubtfully at the door. She obviously wondered whether her English numerals had let her down.

'Three?' she queried.

'Three,' confirmed Rachel decisively.

Anne-Marie went back to the kitchen.

'There must be somebody,' said Adrian. 'It's so ridiculous. If this man — '

'Rachel,' called Mrs Watson, 'what are you plotting out there?'

'Plotting!' echoed Rachel. 'That's just marvellous, isn't it?'

She and Adrian went into the sitting-room, to find the newcomer sitting comfortably in the large armchair facing Mrs Watson, who looked remarkably wide awake and sociable. As Rachel came in he got up politely and waited for her to sit down.

Rachel remained standing.

She said: 'This has gone far enough. You may be able to deceive my grandmother — '

'Whoever may be deceiving me,' snapped Mrs Watson with unexpected fire, 'it's not this young man. He's your husband, Rachel. Whatever are you trying to deny him for?'

'Grandma, if you think I don't know my own husband — '

'Sit down,' said Mrs Watson, 'and let us finish what we were saying.'

Rachel found herself sitting down. Adrian remained standing protectively behind her chair. It was comforting to know that he was there.

'Now,' said Mrs Watson affably; 'what was it you were saying about the canning factory?'

They talked for two or three minutes about the development of a canning factory on some island whose name Rachel did not know, and went on to discuss with typical Danish relish the innumerable things that could be done with herring. When Rachel could endure it no longer, she broke in:

'Grandma . . . '

The old lady glared at her, and pointedly said to the man: 'And your uncle?' For some reason she chuckled. 'I had forgotten. Your uncle — '

He launched suddenly into Danish. Mrs Watson, surprised, put her head on one side as though to catch an echo from long ago; then she bobbed her head like a very old, inquisitive, imitative parrot, and began to chatter along with him, falling back into the tongue of her youth.

Anne-Marie came in with a tray. There were three cups on it. Mrs Watson studied them distantly for a moment, then her gaze came into focus.

'Three cups? There are four of us.'

Anne-Marie glanced uncertainly at Rachel. It was impossible to have an argument in front of the girl. Rachel forced herself to say: 'You had better bring another cup, Anne-Marie.'

When the girl had gone out there was a brief silence. It was filled infuriatingly with the stranger's silent amusement.

Adrian said: 'I still think we are entitled

to an explanation.'

'Yes,' said Mrs Watson sharply. 'There is certainly some need for an explanation. Rachel, why are you trying to repulse your husband?'

It was no good saying that the old woman was vague, that she wasn't in her right mind, that she had no idea what she was talking about. There she sat, and she was waiting to be convinced; and there was still a dogged power in her frail old body.

'Grandma, there has been some awful mistake,' Rachel attempted. 'If you'll give me time to clear it up I'll prove to you that I don't know this man.'

'You'll prove it, will you, indeed? You'll prove that this is not Erik Petersen of Hennesø, whose family I knew when I was a girl? You know about the farm that produces the finest cheese outside the Fynbo and Maribo types?'

'Yes, but — '

'And who told you about the farm and the cheese?'

'Erik. My husband. But this isn't — '

'What about the fish — his uncle's fish?'

Rachel's lips set firmly. She was not going to say another word.

The impostor, as though helping her out, said gently: 'You know I've told you about the small fleet that my grandfather started, and then how we set up the canning factory. And the story about the day when I got caught in the storm off the headland, and had to — '

'No!' cried Rachel in spite of herself.

'No?' he queried. 'You mean you haven't heard that story?'

'I've heard it,' she said wildly, 'but not from you.'

Mrs Watson stirred irritably in her chair. 'I don't know what your game is, my girl, but you needn't think you're going to shrug your husband off just like that.'

'Grandma, you don't imagine I'd pretend he wasn't my husband if he was? I mean, why — '

'I don't know what your game is,' her grandmother repeated. 'But I don't like it. I know that this is your husband. We've been talking, and I know that this is Erik Petersen.'

'But you never saw him,' protested Rachel. 'If you'd seen him just after we were married — the man I really married, I mean . . . '

'I invited the two of you to come over to England and see me,' her grandmother pointed our reproachfully. 'But you didn't come.'

'We didn't have time. Erik was drowned.'

'He is a very substantial ghost,' said Mrs Watson.

Rachel pushed herself up from her chair, despairing. It was all incredible. She could see that her grandmother was convinced. This man had told her true stories, and filled in the accurate background of Erik Petersen and his family. And he had known about Rachel herself and those arguments of her brief married life. Everything was right: Erik Petersen, his passport, the name of his home, the details of his grandfather's business, and doubtless all the other things he had discussed with Mrs Watson. All of it true; all of it Erik.

But not *this* Erik!

3

Rachel had met Erik in the May of that year; a life-time ago. In the exhilaration of the Danish spring, the Nordic Historical Conference had been held in Copenhagen, and she had travelled there with her grandfather. There were solemn Swedes, massive Norwegians, eager young scholars, and dour old pedants. There was the reading of abstruse papers, and the internecine warfare of argument.

Hammond Watson had been in the forefront of every argument. From runic stones to the making of swords, from the settlement of the Faroes to the significance of the battle of Stiklestad, there was no topic on which he did not hold decided opinions. The fact that these opinions frequently ran counter to the views propounded by leading historians did not daunt him: in fact, he seemed happiest when launching an attack with what appeared to be inadequate forces behind him. Put up a scholar, and Hammond Watson determined to shoot him down.

He had always been fascinated by the Vikings, yet was equally repelled by them. Although quarrelsome and harsh of tongue himself, he shied away from physical brutality. Rachel had often seen him shudder when discussing some particularly hideous story of the men whose long ships had terrified Europe. But he went on delving and finding out more. He had done years of work in Holland, caught in the spell of the polders and the inlets of that shallow coast, yet Rachel knew that he did not care for the Dutch. He was enslaved by the Nordic and Teutonic world, while at the same time denying its traditions. For some Englishmen, the wogs begin at Calais; for Hammond Watson, the Huns began at Ostend. Yet nothing could tempt his mind away from the bloody history of the Viking scourges along the European coasts.

He was no true scholar, said some of his critics and those he had criticized. His methods were unscientific. He was too impulsive, valued his intuition too highly, was driven on too recklessly by his own perverse enthusiasms.

Not a scholar. Neither, he might have retorted, was Schliemann — and *he* uncovered Troy. But Hammond Watson made no such retort. Schliemann, after all, had been a Hun.

It had been a strange love-hate relationship. And perhaps it had been the same in his marriage to a Danish girl. By the time Rachel was old enough to regard them as human beings rather than as somewhat remote, awe-inspiring elderly relatives, it was impossible to believe that they had ever shared anything. Kirsten Watson, who perhaps had been made for cosy domesticity, stayed in England alone while her celebrated husband excavated at Lindholm, sifted the sands of Jutland through his fingers, and brooded over the mud of Friesland.

In due course Rachel came to know more about Hammond Watson's work than his wife had ever done. She became his secretary and went everywhere with him. She took notes, kept records, and typed up scribbles from the backs of envelopes, cigarette packets, and conference programmes. She looked after train tickets and booked accommodation. She began to learn a great deal about Viking history.

'Self-taught,' said her grandfather approvingly. 'Just like me. The only way to learn!'

Rachel found him wayward and monstrously selfish; but they got on well together. He would decide to visit Denmark, let her make all the bookings, and then change his mind — and then, a day after the cancellations, ask her what the hell she had altered all the arrangements for. If she did not share his eagerness over some new find, he would sulk like a child; but if she enthused too readily over something, he would turn on her and sneer at her naivety. She learned to keep a check on her tongue.

When they first came to Holland to settle down for an intensive study of the new polder Rachel had had visions of great discoveries, not necessarily in her grandfather's specialized field.

'Ships,' she had surmised: 'surely they'll dig up a lot of wrecks — galleons, maybe?'

The Dutch surveyor who had been a particular friend of Hammond Watson's chuckled. 'Spanish treasure ships, you think?'

'Why not? Spain dominated the Netherlands for a long time. There must have been some wrecks.'

The man had shaken his head with irritating certitude. 'We do not expect to find that kind of ship. Mainly there are coastal vessels — fishing smacks, old cargo boats, and fragments of wrecks washed inshore. We do not expect buried treasure.'

'Find me a long ship,' Hammond Watson had said. '*That* would be treasure!'

But it was true that in all their excavations they had found only small craft. Now, looking out over the flat wet floor of the polder, it was hard to believe that any great galleon could still be concealed there.

Rachel and her grandfather often

squabbled, but there was a tough mutual respect between them. She often disapproved of him, but could never imagine being disloyal to him. One either gave one's allegiance to him, or one loathed him.

There were plenty who loathed him.

He had clashed with a Norwegian expert over the precise location of Jomsborg, legendary home of the harshly disciplinarian Jomsvikings. He had demolished a German chauvinist who tried to identify Elbing with vanished Truso. In the interpretation of runic stones he had shattered conclusively, blow by blow, an attempt by one eminent scholar to establish a relationship between the carvings on a Swedish rock and the Christ figure on the Jelling stone in Denmark. At the beginning of each of these campaigns he had appeared to be on uncertain ground. As time went on, his forcefulness had worn his opponents down. Doggedly he had amassed facts to smash their theories. Unwaveringly he had pressed on until they gave up and retreated, not so much denying their original theories as unobtrusively abandoning them. There were many mild, scholarly men who hated Hammond Watson like poison because he had found his way to the truth from what they considered to be the wrong direction.

Hammond Watson was remorseless and ruthless. It was even said that he had caused the death, two years before his own, of the most eminent of all his Danish contemporaries, Hans Ascomann; one of his most dearly cherished theories torn to pieces by Watson, Ascomann had died of a broken heart.

'Decadence,' snorted Watson when the whisper reached him. 'Can you imagine one of the man's ancestors curling up and dying because somebody had said he'd made a mistake? Just shows how a race can decline.'

Asked to write an obituary article on Ascomann, Watson did it with a sort of reverent relish. It was not a matter of damning with faint praise: he praised lavishly, and then with apparent timidity pointed out the feet of clay. There was a lot of acrimonious correspondence as a result. Hammond Watson joined in, and was more acrimonious than any of his attackers.

In his own squeamish way, Rachel always thought, he was essentially a raider — a filibuster. Adapting the physical violence of the Vikings to his own time, he plunged straight into the ranks of the pedants and scattered them with his axe.

The very vigour of the man was endearing. He believed in himself and in his own view of history. He was boisterous with his friends — few as they were — and unrelenting as far as his enemies were concerned. Coming to him from her interminable expensive schooling, Rachel was caught up into his world at once, and was grateful for it.

But there were tracts of boredom. In the winter months in Holland, the wind and rain were interminable. If the two of them went out together on to the polder, sloshing across the mud in gumboots or on wooden slats, the cold bit into her bones and remained there for days on end. If her grandfather went out alone or with one of the young assistants he periodically adopted and then abandoned, he would leave her to her own devices all day in that clean but soulless house, and the evenings would be spent in elucidating his chaotic notes. At conferences she would sometimes have gloriously sunny days to herself; sometimes she would have to stay in her hotel room while rain slid down the window.

In Copenhagen that May the sun shone.

She had visited the green-spired city several times before with her grandfather, but only in winter or on their way to some remoter place. This was the first chance she had ever had of seeing those copper spires radiant against a blue sky, and of sensing the enduring vitality of the modern Dane. It was an unsettling experience.

There were few notes to be taken or typed up. Most of the speeches at the conference were already printed in various languages, and she merely filed them away when her grandfather brought them back from the various sessions he attended. She went with him to a couple of the typical Danish light suppers which lasted until two o'clock in the morning, and attended a special ballet performance of an old folk-tale which she found charming and he found nauseating. Apart from that, she was very much on her own. For the first two days, that was.

On the evening of the second day, strolling back in the bright evening from the music and gaiety of Tivoli's exhilarating gardens, she noticed a tall, broad-shouldered young Dane watching her as she entered the hotel. There was nothing furtive about his gaze. He leaned against the railings of the churchyard facing the hotel entrance, and stared frankly and appreciatively at her.

Anywhere else it might have been disturbing. Here she had already learned to take such things for granted. The Danes loved to stare. They loved to sit in their outdoor restaurants and watch the passers-by, or settle on a seat in Tivoli and smile — the men sizing up the women, the women happily returning smiles and making it clear that they were by no means averse to being spoken to. Rachel found herself half-smiling at this rather impressive young man.

When she found him there the next

morning as she emerged into the sunshine, her smile was unrestrained. The Copenhagen atmosphere made all things reasonable and inoffensive.

During the morning she was not aware of him following her, but as she went through Tivoli past the sparkling fountains, looking for somewhere to have a leisurely lunch, he was suddenly beside her.

He said: 'You wish a good lunch?'

'That's what I had in mind,' Rachel agreed.

'You will lunch with me.'

She felt no instinctive withdrawal. Here, in spring, nobody took things seriously. It was all part of the spirit of the place — the explosive irresponsibility she had witnessed here the previous evening, the pagan energy that throbbed through the city now that the sun was shining. Visitors could take as much of it as they chose — rather as a sunbather on a Riviera shore could lie in the sun for as long as she thought advisable — and then go away. If you judged correctly you would not be scorched. Invigorated, not burnt; it required only a little self-discipline.

Over lunch he was attentive, yet boyishly awkward in the most delightful way. 'You have not seen the Mermaid? Ah . . . a tourist trap, they say, but she is so beautiful. You will see her with me. The sweet herring on that plate — you like it? Let me pass you some . . . ' While he talked, his blue eyes took in all the details of her face, and then fell acquisitively to her breasts. The sun, warm on her throat, seemed to be allied with him, as ardent as he was.

The little trucks delivered crates of lager to the restaurants. Water was sprayed over the paths and the gravel. The fountains kept up their cool, soothing sound, and the chimes of the City Hall tower dropped through the trees.

Rachel said: 'It's funny what this place does to you. I feel as though I have all the time in the world — as though I'm never, never going to leave.'

'Do you have to leave?'

'Sooner or later.'

'It must be later.'

She laughed, and he answered her with a flash of a smile. Rachel looked round, at the tables and the flowers and the food and the façade of the concert hall through the fountains; but he stared only at her.

It was flattering, but too serious. He could not be so serious at a first meeting. This, at any rate, did not belong: it was not carefree enough, not a part of the city's healthy irresponsibility.

'You are English,' he said.

'Yes.'

'I wish to know your name.'

Rachel hesitated. He leaned towards her as though to draw the name out of her.

She said: 'Rachel Watson.'

'I am Erik Petersen.'

He took her to see the Mermaid, sitting nostalgically on her rock. The harbour flashed and sparked with the brightness of the sun. Erik took her arm as they walked. He had a firm, possessive hand. He was incredibly tense and vital. Rachel found herself caught up into an evening of food, drink, and dancing. At two o'clock in the morning there were still people in the streets, and cafés were still filled with music.

The next day he took her up the coast to Klampenborg and they drove in a horse-drawn carriage through the deer park. He kissed her. Why not? It wasn't serious. It was all part of an exhilarating trip that had become, for Rachel, an unexpected holiday. Her grandfather gave her a few scribbled notes each morning, and she typed them up within half an hour. Then she was ready to go out.

'What are you looking so pleased with yourself for?' Hammond Watson demanded on the fourth morning. 'Found yourself a blond beast?'

'I'm enjoying myself,' said Rachel.

'I'd like to meet him.' But he was really too engrossed with the lectures and discussions to mean what he said. He did not meet Erik until the day when Erik came to talk to him about the wedding.

Rachel never quite understood how it had all happened. It came on her too quickly. There was the sun, and the breeze off the sea; there were lights and laughter and the insistence of Erik's mouth — insistent on hers, insistent when he spoke and told her that she was going to marry him, she must marry him.

When the fortnight of the conference was over Hammond Watson intended to stay on for private meetings and work in the local archives. In that third week, breathless and amazed, Rachel found herself marrying Erik.

Contributing to her amazement was the fact that her grandfather liked Erik. He was normally suspicious of any young man brash enough to come near, and one might have expected him to burst out in a rage at the thought of losing his grand-daughter to an impetuous young Dane. But the two of them got on together at once. Erik's charm was irresistible — if you could call it charm. He came out bluntly with the statement that he proposed to marry Rachel, and there was something in his manner that appealed to Hammond Watson. Erik's very impertinence was a mark in his favour.

'There's a thrusting young man,' he said approvingly. 'He'll keep you in your place, my girl.'

'Don't sound so vindictive,' Rachel protested.

Her grandfather roared with laughter. 'You need someone strong to cope with you.' He raised his thick black eyebrows fiercely. 'You've been brought up in a hard school — with me. It'll take a real man to carry on the tradition. No ordinary little weakling would be capable of standing up to you.'

'You're a conceited old rogue,' said Rachel.

'I've every justification for being so.'

Hammond Watson was even more pleased when he found what Erik's profession was.

'A soil chemist? Perfect. Couldn't be better. Just the man I need to help me in my investigations in Holland. Invaluable when it comes to dating.'

'But I have work,' said Erik. 'I have a job at a research station in Fyn — a new one which I must take up in six or seven weeks' time. That is where we shall live when we are married.'

Rachel wanted the conversation to be brought back on to a more personal plane. Her grandfather turned everything too readily to his own use and his own interests. She said:

'Your parents live near there?'

Erik's face darkened. 'I have no parents.'

'Oh, I'm sorry. I . . . ' She knew so little about him! Knew nothing, really.

'They are alive,' he said bluntly, 'but they are nothing to me. And I am nothing to them. We do not speak.'

'But when they know you're getting married . . . '

'They will not know from me,' he said. 'It would be nothing to them. We shall marry here, and we shall live in Fyn. And they will live on Hennesø, as they have always done. They will stay there.'

His manner denied the possibility of questions. Later, she thought, he would tell her. Later, when they talked about each other, and discovered all there was to know of each other, he would tell her about his mother and father.

'I've been thinking,' announced Hammond Watson.

Erik turned respectfully towards him.

Rachel waited, a trifle apprehensively. Even now she never knew what sort of thing her grandfather was likely to come out with.

He said: 'You're going to have a honeymoon, I suppose? Spend it in Holland — help me for a week or two. Give you something to do in the daytime.'

Rachel opened her mouth to protest, and then was suddenly aware that Erik had stiffened in anticipation. He might almost have been waiting for this. He put his arm round her. 'What do you think?' He took it for granted she would say yes.

'Not the whole time.' Already she was giving way. 'Really, I do think that I'm entitled to at any rate a week away from bones, pots, and grave ornaments. A week in . . . well, what about Austria?'

'What about it?' jibed her grandfather.

'I've always had an idea . . . always thought that when I got married I'd like to have a week or two in Austria.'

'Sentimental music and cream cakes?'

'It's just what I've always thought,' she said doggedly.

Erik laughed and made a broad,

magnificent gesture with his arm as though to sweep her off her feet and toss her into the air.

'If that is what you want . . . '

'Oh, give the girl her romantic week,' agreed Hammond Watson.

The two of them made it sound like a concession made by adults to an awkward child. 'Let's get it over with' — Erik did not say it in so many words, but she felt that that summed up his mood. When he talked to her grandfather she could tell how much they looked forward to being together. They were two of a kind: contemptuously self-centred, self-assured . . . and ruthless.

At the last moment she ought to have asked herself why she was marrying Erik. But he overwhelmed her, rushed her along, gave her no time to ask questions. His mere physical presence was so powerful and immediate that argument was impossible. The panic that fluttered at the back of her mind was not strong enough to take hold of her and snatch her away from under his spell.

They were married in Copenhagen,

and flew to Austria. They stayed at a hotel in the centre of Bad Aussee, shut away in an exquisite maze of twisting narrow streets, with the grim peaks of the Totes Gebirge visible between the roof-tops; and there the panic flared up and became strong at last — too late.

Erik used her savagely. When he made love to her it was done furiously and wordlessly, as though he were wreaking some terrible revenge. He asked for no response from her, and there were no more of the outrageous, exuberant compliments he had paid her when he drove her towards marriage. Now that he possessed her he seemed to feel no need to say anything flattering or gentle. His laughter took on a new note — a frightening, inexplicable note of triumph.

'Erik' — trapped in his arms, bruised and pounded by his body, she asked the most banal of all questions in desperation — 'do you love me?'

He would not speak. He simply laughed.

In the daytime she tried to soak up the beauty of the valley, with its wayward lanes, so soft and soothing. But Erik was curt and unenthusiastic. He rejected the beauty around them. She could not share it with him. Once or twice he mentioned her grandfather and the work that was waiting in Holland. It was the only topic of conversation that aroused any interest in him. She knew how anxious he was to get to Stevinstad.

It was almost as though he had married her only to get close to her grandfather. But that made no sense. Nothing about him made sense.

It was said that the Danes were erratic. They had a high suicide rate: if things did not go well they killed themselves too readily. But what was there that had not gone well between herself and Erik? He had seemed to hate her the very moment they were married, as though he had been holding in the hatred until then and now could give it full rein.

Had she disappointed him? Shame was a creeping sensation at the back of her neck. But she was not conscious of having failed him. What right had he to be so contemptuous?

Rachel had been brought up in a hard

school of argument. She was not easily defeated. Her grandfather had toughened her. But she had not expected to need the benefit of those experiences in order to deal with the man she loved.

The man she loved . . .

The shock of uncertainty took her breath away. She did not know if she loved him; did not see how she could love anyone who had deliberately, wantonly, made himself remote.

Remote. For sharing a bed with a man and sitting opposite him at meal-times did not necessarily bring him close.

She suffered for three days and nights, then the anger burned up within her.

They were lying beside the Altausseersee, still damp from swimming. He ought to have been beside her, touching her. He ought to have wanted to touch her. Other men who went past them that day, and on other days, had looked at her and obviously thought of what it would be like to touch her. Why should Erik lie there indifferent?

Rachel said: 'Erik — why did you marry me?'

He did not even open his eyes. Calmly he said: 'Because I wanted you.'

'Wanted me?' The lash in her voice ought to have stung him, but still he did not move. 'Wanted me for what?'

'You are my wife,' he murmured.

'I don't feel like your wife. I don't feel as though you know me at all . . . or want to know me. Erik, what's wrong? I've got to know.'

Now he opened his eyes. Slowly he sat up, but he was not looking at her. He stared tranquilly across the lake.

'Wrong?' he said. 'I do not please you?'

'You don't even try,' she cried. 'Why' — she hammered it home again — 'did you marry me?'

Erik rolled over on his side. 'I thought it would be interesting to possess you. Now I possess you . . . so I know what it is like. And now I think it will be interesting to work with your grandfather in Holland.'

The callousness of it caught at her throat. A whimper escaped her, and she could have sworn that Erik derived an immediate satisfaction from it.

'Why are you so cruel?' she whispered. 'What have I done to deserve this?'

'In England there is a translation of those words about . . . how do you say it? . . . the sins of the fathers . . . ' He stopped, then went on quickly, offhandedly: 'I have heard that a honeymoon is a mistake. Women are too excited — excitable. When we live our ordinary lives you will settle down.'

He was not even taking the trouble to sound as though he meant it. She could take it or leave it. She found it impossible to answer back. You could not argue with someone who was not listening and who did not care.

'When we get to Holland,' he concluded lightly, 'perhaps you will be more sensible.'

She could have hit him for that remark — could have scratched him, spat at him, even left him. But she did none of those things. Pride and bewilderment struggled for ascendancy. She crept back inside herself, not knowing what had happened to her or why it had had to happen. Until she found out, she could not fight: she did not know what weapons to use.

In Holland the sun still shone, but the flat land seemed bleak and unwelcoming. She felt an absurd gladness at being back in the house she and her grandfather had come to regard as home; but the gladness was damped by the presence of this interloper — her husband.

Not that she saw much of him. He was very correct with her when her grandfather was present, joking brusquely in a way that Hammond Watson greatly appreciated; but she was chilled by the savage coldness beneath. The two men seemed to be in league against her. The only difference between them was that her grandfather loved her — she knew, in spite of his growls and glares, that he did — and Erik did not. Of that she was wretchedly sure. He did not love her and had never loved her.

Then why had he been so passionately set on marrying her?

She was left as much on her own as she had been when she was single. More so, really, for now her grandfather rarely took her out with him. Erik was his companion

— Erik, whose analyses of soil layers and constituents could establish dates and periods. Hammond Watson, who had employed at least four young men in the past twelve months and then thrown them out, showed every sign of adopting Erik Petersen as a grandson. Rachel had been only an intermediary. This was the relationship the old man had been waiting for. There had been polite, reverent young men whose awe had provoked shouts of derision; there had been young Danish scholars who asked no more than the privilege of working with him; but it took this aggressive, scornful young barbarian to win his heart.

One night, towards the end of the first week in Stevinstad, Rachel awoke to find that Erik was not beside her. She reached out drowsily, and felt that the sheets and blankets had been turned carefully back. She waited, ready to go off to sleep again, yet uneasy. Perhaps she dozed off into a spasmodic dream. Certainly time seemed to pass, but Erik did not come back.

At last she was awake. The room was dark, and there was no promise of daylight beyond the window. She sat up in bed.

The silence was uncanny. There was no wind, and tonight there was no sound of the sea. Everything was still.

Then there was a movement downstairs.

Rachel pushed her hands down against the bed, and sat tensely. She hardly breathed. The sound came again. Somebody was moving cautiously about. Trying to locate the sound, she realized that it must come from her grandfather's study.

She got out of bed and slid her feet into slippers. They were soft and silent. The house was a new one, so that the stairs did not creak as she went down. The door of the study fitted perfectly, so that no light shone underneath it.

Rachel stood outside the room, one hand poised above the door handle. She waited. Silence was absolute again. Had she imagined it; or had he heard her coming?

Then there was the faint rustle of paper. It was followed by an equally faint

68

squeak that she recognized as the sound made by the drawer in the desk at which she did most of her work.

Her knees were trembling. She was afraid — but not afraid in the way she would have been of an ordinary burglar. The man in there, she was sure, was her husband. And she was afraid of him and of what she might find out. But it wasn't the sort of fear that would make her call for help or stay out.

She turned the handle, and went in.

Erik was sitting at the desk, turning over papers under the small lamp there. His mouth was tight, and his brow was furrowed by impatience. When Rachel came in he looked up. There was no surprise in his face. He simply threw the papers down with a muttered curse, and leaned back in the chair.

Rachel said: 'What are you doing down here?'

'Looking through the records,' he said blandly.

'You've got no business to turn things over like that. My grandfather's confidential notes — '

'There's nothing he wants to keep secret from me,' said Erik. And then, oddly accusing, he said: 'Is there?'

'If he wants you to see anything,' said Rachel, 'he'll show it to you himself.'

'I couldn't sleep. I was turning over some of our findings in my head, and I had to come down and check a point or two.'

'I shall ask him whether he approves of your . . . nosing into things.' Abruptly she remembered Poul, one of her grandfather's helpers who had been just that bit too assiduous, and who had also made himself too readily at home in this study. She said: 'There was one young man before you who started rooting about. Grandad threw him out the next day — packed him off to Denmark and threatened to have him completely banished fro — '

'Your grandfather,' Erik interrupted, 'will not treat me like that. He often wakes up in the night himself and comes down here. He has told me. He will understand.'

His confidence was unassailable. And

well it might be. Rachel felt left out: she belonged to him, but he didn't seem to want her.

She burst out: 'Is this the only reason you married me: so that you could worm your way into my grandfather's good graces, and find out about his work?'

Erik studied her for a second or two. It was almost as though he were about to agree with her: she was sure that he was on the verge of nodding. Then he sneered and waved his hand at her, shooing her away.

'Go back to bed,' he said. 'I will not be long.'

'What's it going to be like,' Rachel cried, 'when we go to live in Denmark — in Fyn? Is it going to go on like this?'

'You do not wish to come with me?' said Erik sourly, provocatively.

'If you're going to be like this all the time — '

'I am sorry,' he said abruptly. He smiled, and came towards her. All at once his arms were round her, and he was kissing her. She struggled to free herself; then tried to answer, to return his kiss.

'Rachel, I am sorry,' he murmured into her ear, his mouth brushing across her cheek. 'I am a fool. It is just that I have been so impressed by meeting your grandfather — I am not used to great men, it is strange for me . . . But I must not neglect you, must I?'

'Erik . . . if only you'd talk to me. Tell me what's wrong.'

Even as she spoke she knew that she was wasting her time. She did not believe a word of his apology. She did not believe in the pressure of his hands now, or in the movement of his mouth. He was soothing her down because he didn't want trouble: he was playing her along, that was all.

But why?

Hopelessly she said: 'Erik, is there something that's hurt you — something you're afraid to talk about?'

'I am not afraid to talk,' he said gently, kissing her ear. It meant nothing. She felt empty. She could not respond to this insincere mockery.

'Your parents?' she tried. 'Something to do with your mother and father?'

'We do not speak about my mother and

72

father,' he said coldly. Now his grip on her relaxed. 'My father,' he breathed, more to himself than to her. When they moved apart his face was set and ugly with that bewildering hostility.

Rachel turned away. She did not want him to see the tears that were coming into her eyes.

He said in a level tone: 'Go back to bed, Rachel. I will come in a few minutes.'

But she had fallen asleep before he came to bed.

The next day she determined to make him speak. When he tried to go into the museum to help her grandfather arrange some new additions, Rachel said:

'I want to talk to you.'

He frowned. 'I do not like too much talk.'

'Either you treat me like a rational human being, and tell me about yourself, and what sort of future we're going to have,' Rachel persisted, 'or I'll make a scene. A real scene. One that'll wake even my grandfather up. He may be selfish, but I do know how to get my own way with him now and then. If I insist on having you to myself for a day or two, I'll get you. And if I ask you certain questions outright, in front of him, he'll get a bit disturbed if you don't answer. Well — what's it to be?'

Erik sighed. 'They told me Englishwomen were fond of arguing. They cannot rest — that is what I was told. It is true.'

'I want to get out of this house,' said Rachel. 'We'll go for a walk along the wall.'

It was a bright but blustery day. She bent against the wind. Her husband ought to have taken her arm. She ought to be able to lean on him. But he ignored her. He strode along, his head down, making no concessions to her.

Rachel said: 'Do you think we can ever be happy?'

'Happy? Women today speak too much of happiness. It is best to live and not ask too many questions.'

'But you wanted to marry me. You said things to me then that . . . that . . . ' She faltered. It was incredible that he should have been so ardent then, so rich with promises, and now should be such an icy creature.

Erik said: 'That was a mistake. I should have behaved as my ancestors did. When we wanted Englishwomen in the old days we sailed our ships across to your coasts and took what we needed. We tore open your menfolk and spread their ribs out. And then we raped the women, and if we found them worthy we took them away with us.'

'How can you get such pleasure out of the thought of cruelty?' she said. 'It *is* pleasure, isn't it?'

He twisted his head away from the wind to glance at her. Not for the first time, he looked accusing. 'There are many kinds of cruelty,' he said. 'Murder and rape are not always the worst. Some men have done things . . . ' Then he jerked his head away again and they went on walking.

Spending too long on the wall, one could get dizzy. The road went on and on in its slow, implacable curve. After you had walked for fifteen minutes the road seemed to rear up into the air, and then you had the sensation of falling towards it, rolling up it. The sea pulled on one side; the polder was waiting on the other.

Rachel drew closer to Erik. He gave no indication of having noticed this.

She said: 'I've asked you this already, but you haven't answered. I think you ought to. I think you ought to tell me about your parents — why you won't speak to them, why they weren't invited to the wedding, or even told about it.'

'We do not speak about my parents,' he said. And then, before she could pursue the matter, he started to pour out an interminable story about other relatives. He told her about his grandfather, who had started a small fishing fleet and founded a canning factory which was still run by the family. He dredged up trivial stories about his youth, and about uncles and aunts. This was what she had wanted him to do — it was what people in love did, trying to tell everything and make the picture complete. Yet now she was still unsatisfied. There was no warmth in the way he told these stories. None of it mattered to him. Once or twice she even felt that he was inventing them, just to keep her quiet. Once more she was a child and he was an adult, telling her tales to pacify her.

When they returned to the house, she realized that she was still no wiser. It was not that he was elusive: he simply refused to meet her. Speech was a barrier rather than a communication.

The prospect of the future was terrifying. Life could not go on like this, stretching dizzily and interminably ahead of her like that road along the wall. She could not believe in a future with Erik; and somehow he gave the impression of not believing in it either.

Something had to happen.

When the accident came it seemed that everything must have been leading up to it. There had to be an answer, and this was it.

Already there had been a couple of summer storms this year. They were not frightening down here, where the new wall still looked very sure of itself. You could not envisage a crack in this dam, and the water pouring through. A few miles to the north, though, at the junction of the new polder and the old enclosing dam, there was often a seething confusion of water over the sluices. The threat was not a major one, but the area was not the most comfortable place for anyone who did not understand the tides and the control of the fresh-water lake level.

Hammond Watson knew the place well enough. He had been there many times before, taking a canoe from one side of the inland lake to the other. A site on the northern shore had produced several good finds, and he was in the habit of going back there from time to time to see what the workmen on an agricultural project there had turned up.

This time he took Erik with him. It was not established quite what happened to them, for there were no witnesses. Perhaps the blinding rain had come on them so suddenly that they had been unable to paddle in the right direction: they had let themselves smash against the sluice without knowing it was there until too late. Perhaps they had lost a paddle, or perhaps Hammond Watson, stubborn as always, had insisted on going too close to the storm-whipped cross-currents because some wild theory had taken possession of his mind — one of those theories that had to be followed up at once, without time for thought and planning. Whatever it was, it meant death.

The boat was found, shattered. Hammond Watson was found, washed up two miles away.

Erik Petersen had not been found. It was just possible that he had been sucked out to sea through the discharging sluice, though the experts said it was unlikely. There was still time for him to drift in to shore from the lake. Perhaps the weeds had trapped him. Perhaps . . .

It was all speculation now. Just as their possible life together was now only a matter for speculation.

Rachel had written to Erik's parents at Hvidfelt on Hennesø, telling them of the death. They had not replied. It was part of a chilling, inhuman mystery that would now never be solved.

So, at least, she had thought until this

impostor who called himself Erik Petersen appeared on the scene. He had an uncanny knowledge of what had happened to Erik and herself, and of Erik's background. If he knew that much, he must know more — must know everything. And he must speak. She wanted to know the reason for his crazy pretence, and the reason would inevitably be bound up with the reasons for Erik's behaviour during their brief marriage. She had to find out. He had to tell her.

4

Mrs Watson yawned.

The tall Dane was at once solicitous. He went across to her chair and put his strong hand over her frail one.

'I am so sorry,' he said. 'I have tired you. I have talked too much.'

The old lady shook her head. 'It has been good to hear the things you have to say. It has been a long time since I talked like this.'

It seemed a good opportunity for getting her out of the room for a short rest. And while she was out, something might be done about tackling this impostor. Rachel said:

'Grandma, why not go and lie down for an hour? We'll call you when dinner's ready.'

'We will have dinner,' said her grandmother firmly, 'and then we will all go to bed early.'

She had drawn strength from the

conversation. The presence of this young man had given her new life, and she seemed anxious to assert herself. Rachel and Adrian had sat in silence while those other two exchanged stories and reminiscences. Meeting, as it were, vicariously through mutual acquaintances, they sounded as though they had known each other for years. Every now and then they slipped into Danish. Rachel noticed that it was always the man who first edged them into this language. Was it because there was a chance of their saying something on certain topics that he did not wish Rachel to hear?

For a wild moment she wondered if her grandmother were mixed up in this plot, whatever it might be. There was no doubt that it was a plot of some sort. No other theory made sense; and even this one was mad enough, heaven knows.

Adrian stirred. Rachel glanced at him hopefully. He had been sunk into glowering depression, and she had known — a painful knowledge — that he was not sure of her. She could hardly blame him. It was all very well to expect a man to trust you, but in the face of this other man's amazing plausibility, how could you condemn anyone who doubted? Now he was about to make some move.

He said: 'What have you been doing with yourself this last couple of months?'

Mrs Watson pursed her lips and made a disapproving sucking noise between them. Then, grudgingly, she said: 'Mm. I think you do owe us that much of an explanation, young man.'

Rachel sighed. Relief could surely not be long in coming now.

The man who called himself Erik Petersen walked slowly away from the old lady's chair. He touched the wall, as though trying to recognize it through his fingers. When he turned back towards them he looked very grave.

'They tell me,' he said, 'that I went back to Denmark and worked in an office there. I was good at my job, although I remembered nothing of my own life.'

The noise between Mrs Watson's lips became agitated.

'You mean you . . . you lost your memory?'

'Until I saw the announcement about the unveiling of the memorial — '

'You poor boy.'

Rachel and Adrian exchanged glances. Adrian was wary. Rachel stiffened. It was obvious to her that the man was not telling the truth. It was too glib and at the same time too contrived. She glared at him, trying to force an acknowledging glint of amusement into his eyes. But he was ready for her.

'Amnesia!' she said scornfully.

'A complete blank,' he nodded. 'And then — purely by chance — I saw the announcement of the ceremony. I could not understand what had happened to me. I remembered everything — but not how I had passed those weeks, and not how I had got back to Denmark. It took me some time to find the reference in the Danish papers to the accident. Mr Watson's name was given a certain amount of prominence, but there was no more than a bare reference to Erik Petersen. He was nobody — he attracted no attention!'

'I don't believe a word of it.'

'Rachel!' Her grandmother spat the

word out like a shout of abuse. 'If you cannot behave yourself I must insist that you leave the room. I will not have your husband distressed by this deplorable exhibition. Simply because you wish to marry another man — '

'Grandma, you have no right to make such an accusation.'

'You want to marry another man,' repeated Mrs Watson with a venomous glance at Adrian, 'and you're furious because your proper husband has come home. As though it will do you any good to pretend, when the whole thing can be settled through legal channels — a mere matter of marriage register and witnesses.'

Rachel's cheeks burned. She cried: 'I'm only too glad to put it to a test like that. At once.'

'Don't talk nonsense, child. We are marooned out here in this terrible little outpost — '

'We've got the car,' said Adrian.

'I'm willing to try for a night plane to Copenhagen,' seethed Rachel.

'Well, I'm not. And I want no nonsense. Nothing done behind my back.

I am very tired, and I want a good dinner and an early night. We will all sleep on the matter, and tomorrow it may be that wiser counsels will have prevailed.'

Rachel said: 'I hope you don't imagine — '

'Perhaps you will send for Anne-Marie and order dinner.'

It was an incredible meal. Rachel ate automatically, but tasted nothing. Adrian tackled his food grimly: he tried to keep his 'no-nonsense' expression in place, but whenever he looked at the newcomer it tended to slip. The intruder himself ate heartily, commenting on the food and making the smoothest of polite conversation with Mrs Watson.

Mrs Watson ate more than was usual with her. The sea air, the talk, the stimulation of this man's presence: all of them taken together had provided her with an appetite.

'How long are we proposing to stay here?' asked the man.

Rachel choked on a mouthful. *We . . .* She began to splutter: 'There's no question of your — '

'I look forward to being back in England three days from now,' said Mrs Watson.

'In that case, you and I' — he turned towards Rachel — 'will soon be able to travel to Fyn. They were very kind about my non-appearance. The job is still there for me. Or would you prefer us to go somewhere else, start a different sort of life?'

'I've no intention of starting any sort of life with you.'

He smiled at her. It was an utterly frank, quite unexpectedly warm smile. He was a man who could be gay, warm, sympathetic . . .

Rachel smacked down hard on her own thoughts. Not with her he couldn't!

Her feelings obviously showed in her face. He let the smile linger for a moment, then turned back to Mrs Watson. The warmth was still there when he spoke to the old lady. He was being genuinely charming to her, and with every word you could sense what an entertaining person he might be to know. A Dane without a dark side, thought

Rachel, in spite of herself.

But with a perverse sense of humour as well. A sense of humour that, she assured herself, could be as cruel as anything that her husband Erik had shown her. Already it was cruel. This taunting act of his was cruel in itself.

'Well,' said Mrs Watson with profound satisfaction at the end of the meal, 'an early dinner I said, and early to bed. We will have no coffee — it keeps me awake nowadays. If the gentlemen wish to have a brandy before going to bed — '

'Grandma,' Rachel broke in; 'it's not a question of the gentlemen having brandy and going to bed. It's a question of one of them going home.'

Mrs Watson got to her feet. The stranger was at once behind her chair, moving it away as she shuffled sideways and came down the table.

She said: 'This was your husband's home for a short time. Now that he is back it can be his home until he takes you away to wherever it is you finally decide to go.'

'This is monstrous!' said Adrian.

'Clothes?' said Mrs Watson imperiously.

'The usual things — toothbrush and so on?'

'Everything's gone,' snapped Rachel. 'Sold, given away, or burnt.' She enjoyed the savagery of saying it.

'You were certainly precipitate,' said her grandmother. 'If I were your husband I am not at all sure I would want to come back to such a woman. However, he has chosen to come back, and you will kindly try to observe some of the proprieties in my presence.'

The man who pretended to be Petersen said: 'It must be a bit of a shock to my wife that I should have reappeared so suddenly. Perhaps it was tactless of me — '

'You have every right to come back to her,' said Mrs Watson imperiously.

'Naturally. But it might have been better if I had given her some warning. As it is, she is rather startled. It will be better if we do not share the same room tonight.'

Rachel gasped. 'Not tonight,' she spluttered, 'and not any other night!'

'Your delicate feelings do you credit, my boy,' said Mrs Watson. 'Though why

89

you should pander to her silliness . . . '
She shrugged, and left it at that.

'I can sleep on the couch in the study.'
He went to the door. 'If you will excuse
me, I will get my brief-case. I left it in the
hall. It contains . . . my toothbrush.'

As soon as he was out of the room,
Rachel threw herself forward and kneeled
beside her grandmother.

'Grandma,' she implored her, 'please
listen. Please believe me. I don't know
this man. I swear I don't.'

'You have amnesia as well?' said Mrs
Watson coldly.

'Do you think I could look my own
husband in the face and pretend not to
recognize him — if he really were my
husband? Do you think I could keep up
an act like this?'

'It is just as plausible,' said Mrs Watson,
'as the idea of his pretending to be your
husband. What reason would *he* have?'

'That's what I want to find out. But
please believe me.'

The old lady looked disturbed. She moved
uneasily in her chair. Then she shook her
head, as though to brush cobwebs away.

'I'm too tired to think clearly. I must talk to you — but not now. Tomorrow we will settle down and discuss all this.' Her eyes were glazed with drowsiness, but there was a spasmodic wakeful flicker in them as she looked past Rachel at Adrian. 'I cannot fathom your motives, Rachel,' she muttered. 'I trust that in the morning, after a good sleep, you will be prepared to enlighten me.'

'But, Grandma — '

'It is time for bed,' said Mrs Watson.

Rachel sent for Anne-Marie, and the two of them escorted the old lady upstairs to bed. She had gone very limp; the liveliness provoked by the newcomer was draining rapidly away. The day had exhausted her, and she would sleep.

Rachel was conscious of a similar weariness. She longed to be in bed. When she went slowly downstairs, Adrian was pacing up and down the room.

He said: 'Look here, I'm going to sit up all night. I don't fancy — '

He broke off as the Dane came in, smiling affably.

'Mrs Watson has finished in the

bathroom?' he said. 'Good. I will go up.'

They listened to his footsteps going up the stairs. Then Adrian went on:

'I don't know what game this maniac is up to, but I'm not taking any chances.'

'Adrian, I shall be all right. Really. We'll all go to bed, and in the morning perhaps we'll be able to think clearly. Right now I'm dazed — simply dazed.'

'I couldn't sleep if I thought of that character prowling round.'

His baffled anger did Rachel a world of good. She looked at Adrian's jutting chin, and wanted to laugh and say something warm and affectionate at the same time. Impulsively she stopped him in his pacing, and put her face up to his. Startled, he looked into her eyes for a moment. Then he kissed her — awkwardly, as though it had never occurred to him before that he was ever likely to do such a thing.

Rachel said: 'Adrian, you're sweet. But you do too much for me. I'm not going to have you sitting up all night. I'll lock my door.'

'But — '

'If I need help,' she said gently, 'I'll

scream. Very loudly!'

Adrian looked undecided. He stood there listening, waiting for the stranger to come downstairs. When the footsteps returned the two of them were tense and silent.

The door opened. The Dane's head came round it.

'Good night,' he said cheerfully. 'Do not worry about me. I shall be most comfortable on the couch.'

'That's one thing, anyway,' said Rachel with some satisfaction, after the door had closed again. 'He *won't* be most comfortable on the couch.'

Finally she persuaded Adrian that there was no need for him to carry out his promised vigil. Whatever the intruder's game was it did not seem to threaten violence. They were not all going to be murdered in their beds.

Rachel locked her door. She felt very foolish as she did so. It seemed prim — or melodramatic: she couldn't decide which. The whole thing was so ridiculous. But she knew that she would not have slept if the door had been left unlocked.

Even as it was, she lay awake for a long

time. Her tangled thoughts turned into vague dreams. She sank into fitful sleep, and found herself fishing Erik's body from a vast lake, going through his pockets and taking out a clean, undamaged passport. Then, as soon as she turned her back, he was there again — alive. He came towards her, and the face was no longer Erik's, but that of this man who also called himself Erik.

Her foot slipped over the edge of the lake. She fell six inches . . . and awoke with a jump, her heart lurching.

Why should anyone carry out such an imposture?

She tried to think up some logical story that would explain it all, but in her half-waking state she muttered nonsensical phrases over and over again.

Below her, something moved. In the study, beneath her bedroom, there was the faint restlessness of somebody walking about. It was not a sound: just the awareness of movement.

Abruptly Rachel remembered another night, all those weeks ago, when she had lain in this bed alone and her husband had explored the study in the hours of darkness. Now there was another man down there — a man supposedly sleeping on the couch, but in reality examining the place. Not that there was much for him to see: the treasures which Hammond Watson had reclaimed from the sea-bed were nearly all packaged and docketed ready for transfer to the museum or other institutions with a claim on them.

Rachel swung herself out of bed and poked her feet into her slippers. She opened the door cautiously and went along the passage. There was no sound from the other bedrooms. She was glad that this was a new house, with no creaking floorboards or stair-treads. Then memory tossed up another fragment. She remembered thinking that, feeling just like that, on the previous occasion. It was a crazy repetition, an echo from the past.

Outside the study she hesitated, as she had hesitated once before. Then she opened the door and went in.

The light was on. He was edging from one package to another, studying them as though longing to be able to see the contents through the wrappings. When Rachel came in he swung round, not appearing in the least embarrassed. For one frightened moment she thought she would see the real Erik's face — it was all so much like last time. But it was the newcomer, dressed in green pyjamas and with his raincoat draped over his shoulders. He raised one hand in a casual sort of greeting.

'So you could not sleep? I thought you would find it difficult.'

'You've got a nerve,' said Rachel. 'What are you doing now? What business have you to pry into these things?'

'Having given your grandfather so much help, I don't feel I ought to be treated as — '

'Stop it!' Rachel's voice rose, then she checked it. She did not want to bring Adrian down. Somehow she felt that if she were to drag the truth out of this man, she would have to do it on her own, without help and without an audience. She said, quietly but urgently: 'You never worked with my grandfather. You know that perfectly well. What are you doing here . . . why are you putting up this pretence . . . what do you want?'

'Such a lot of questions,' he smiled.

'Provide some answers,' she shot back at him.

He did not reply at once. Instead, he put his head on one side and studied a label on one of the packages.

'Shards,' he murmured absently. 'How exciting. And what is this? Fragment of an axe-head. Amsterdam. Lucky for Amsterdam. No dates given, though?'

'The material is catalogued,' said Rachel stiffly, 'and there are details inside each package.'

He flicked a corner of brown paper with his fingernail. It gave out an explosive sound.

'I am sorry if I woke you up,' he said. 'I could not sleep. The couch is not so very comfortable. And I was thinking about you.'

She said: 'Who are you?'

'Erik Petersen,' he said.

'You can't keep this up much longer.'

He glanced at her almost shyly. 'No,' he said. 'No, perhaps not.'

'You mean — '

'I mean that even the most insensitive husband knows when he is not wanted. Our Danish divorce laws are very easy. We must come to an agreement, I suppose.'

Rachel took a deep breath. She had to keep calm and to keep quiet. She said levelly: 'All right, if you *are* Erik — '

'Ah, you're coming round!'

'I am not coming round,' she snapped. 'But just for the sake of argument — just to show you up as the fake you are — if you're Erik, why did you stay away so long after the accident? I don't believe the amnesia story. Did you . . . ' The question stuck in her throat. If the answer were yes, she was being mad to ask it. But if it goaded him into some revelation, it was a chance that must be taken. 'Did you,' she asked, 'kill my grandfather?'

It rocked him. She could have sworn that he looked reproachful.

He said: 'No, certainly I did not kill your grandfather. Do I look like a murderer?'

'I don't know what you look like — apart from the fact that you don't look like my husband.' He was motionless. She tried to drive her anguish home, to keep at him until he weakened. 'If you are really Erik, how do you explain the fact that I don't know you? You don't believe my grandmother, do you? You can see I'm not acting. This is real to me. It's important. I know that I've never seen you before in my life — and you know it, too. How could you possibly be Erik? How could I behave like this if you were really my husband come back from the dead?'

He sat down on the couch. Rachel stood above him. She sensed that he was retreating. She folded her arms and looked down on him.

He raised his head, and there was a puzzled, uneasy look in his eyes. Once again she saw how his resemblance to Erik was only a superficial one. Erik would never have been capable of showing that self-doubt, that look almost of pleading.

To her astonishment he said: 'I'm beginning to feel ashamed.'

'I should think so, too.'

'It seemed so . . . so possible. Ironical, and possible. Inevitable, even.'

'What did?' she urged him. 'Tell me.'

He forced a wry smile. 'It started out as a game . . .'

The door opened. Adrian stood in the opening, his woollen dressing-gown wrapped round him.

He said: 'Rachel — you promised me you were going to lock your door.'

'I locked it,' she said impatiently. 'Then I heard a noise down here, so I came down.'

'I appear to have disturbed both of you,' said the Dane.

Rachel put out one hand to him beseechingly. She could tell that he already regretted having said as much as he had done. He was retreating; he was going to escape her.

'Adrian,' she cried, 'we were just talking. I was trying to get at the truth.'

'I'd sooner you did it when I was present,' he said. He moved into the room and took her arm. 'Now will you go to bed? We can all talk in the morning.'

'It will be much better then,' agreed the

Dane — too readily, too obviously relieved.

Rachel let herself be guided out of the room. At the foot of the stairs she tried to shake herself free, but Adrian held her firmly and masterfully.

'You silly little idiot,' he said. It was not a term of affection. She felt that he wanted to put her over his knee and smack her. It was rather sweet of him, really. 'What ever possessed you?' he demanded. 'You don't even know what plans the man has — what he's doing here . . . Or do you? Did you have a nice cosy little chat and settle everything between you?'

'What do you mean by settling things between us?'

'I don't know, Rachel. Do you know yourself? If the man isn't your husband, then how could you — '

Now she succeeded in breaking loose. She went quickly upstairs. Adrian came running after her. He caught her up, halfway, just as the door of the study opened below them.

The Dane stared up at them.

'Are you all right, Rachel?'

'Of course I'm all right.'

'Do you want me to come up to our room and protect you?'

She hurried up the last few steps and along the passage. Adrian hesitated, unable to decide whether to pursue her or whether to go down and start a row with the man who stood below, taunting them. By the time he had made up his mind, Rachel had stormed into her room and slammed the door.

This time she did not trouble to lock it. She felt instinctively that it would not be necessary. When the man had made that last light, insinuating remark, he had laughed; but there had been a wistfulness in his face that was more unsettling than his laughter.

Tomorrow, she vowed — or was it today by this time? — the truth would come out. He had been on the verge of telling her just now.

She was furious with Adrian for intervening at that moment. At the same time it gave her a warm feeling to know that he was there, watchful and ready, determined to defend her and to bully her when she needed it.

Next time they kissed perhaps it would be under more favourable circumstances. She must try to engineer it that way.

Furious because your proper husband has come home ... Mrs Watson's accusation echoed in her head. But he's not my husband, she silently retorted.

Who is he, then?

At last she slept, but her sleep was churned up by a frenzy of dreams which did nothing to clear her mind. She awoke early, and was glad to be awake. In the daylight she would be more capable of dealing with things.

When she went downstairs, it was to find that the man had gone. He had left a brief note for her.

5

The note had been scribbled quickly. It read:

I am sorry that I upset you. It was not kind of me. If you knew the whole story you would know how unkind it has been, but I did not understand that you were so real. You are too real. It is something which I did not take into consideration. Now it is best for me to go. I will not trouble you again. Give my respects to Mrs Watson.
Erik Flemming Petersen

Rachel showed it to Adrian. He read it through a couple of times.

'The man was a maniac,' he said at last. 'What on earth do you suppose he means by 'the whole story'?'

'That's what I want to know.'

'We'll never find out now.'

Rachel took the sheet of paper back.

She was not so sure. Somehow she had to find out. She could not let it rest now; she could not go through life with that weird, unexplained episode always nagging at her thoughts.

She said: 'How did he get away so early? There isn't any transport. Did he have a car of his own?'

Adrian shrugged. 'I've no idea. Probably not. He'd have had more luggage than that brief-case if he had brought his car along here. Maybe he walked to the workings, where they're building up the rear of the dike. He could have got a lift back to town from there on one of the lorries. Anyway, he's gone.'

Rachel said: 'And I'm going after him.'

'Rachel, for goodness' sake . . . '

'He says he won't trouble me again; but can't you see that just the thought of him will always trouble me. He knows things about Erik and myself that he can't possibly know. There must be an explanation. I'll never feel free — I won't even feel absolutely *safe*, if you know what I mean — until I have the explanation.'

'I know it must be exasperating, but you can't go chasing off after him. You don't know where he's going, for one thing.'

'I shall go to Hennesø,' said Rachel flatly.

Her mind was made up. She had no intention of being argued out of it. Oddly enough, her grandmother, when she came down, agreed with her. Mrs Watson was very disappointed to find that the visitor had gone, and gone in such peculiar circumstances. She regarded it as Rachel's duty to pursue her husband and ask him what he was playing at: indeed, she showed positive approval because it seemed that Rachel's interest was in itself an admission that the man was really her husband.

'Quite apart from visiting the island,' Rachel reasoned with Adrian, 'I can do a lot of work in Copenhagen. There are all the details of Grandad's bequests to the National Museum. I could even take some of the smaller items with me — the bracelets, for example.' As the bits of the plan fell neatly into shape, she could almost persuade herself that she had intended to have a few days in Denmark anyway. 'There are several things to be wound up there. I can get it all done, and then go straight home to England. That is' — it dawned on her that she was rather taking things for granted — 'if you don't mind taking Grandma back the day after tomorrow, as we planned.'

Adrian showed a marked lack of enthusiasm. 'You know how little she likes me . . .'

'Do be a darling.' She was prepared to wheedle outrageously. 'We've got everything packed up here. You can simply hand over to the transport men when they come tomorrow, and then let the curator do a formal take-over before you leave the following morning. It's all arranged.'

'I know,' said Adrian drily. 'I arranged a lot of it myself.'

'Of course you did, darling. I've relied on you so much. And I'm going to rely on you again.'

Ten minutes later she was telephoning van Eck, the long-suffering travel agent in Amsterdam who had arranged so many complicated journeys for her grandfather and herself in the past. He was used to demands for last-minute bookings, but sounded a trifle reproachful that she should still be carrying on in this way after her grandfather's death. A moment later he sounded more than reproachful: downright startled, in fact. It was, he explained, not usual to go nosing into passenger lists on other planes, and it was only as a special favour for an old and valued client . . .

'Yes, yes,' said Rachel sweetly. 'But do find out for me, won't you?'

He found out. When he telephoned back he confirmed that an Erik Flemming Petersen had been a passenger on a jet bound for Copenhagen, leaving half an hour ago. He had been lucky, obtaining the seat on a cancellation. Rachel would have to go via Hamburg. And she would be well advised to leave without delay if she hoped to report at Schiphol on time. He would have all her tickets ready for her at the airport. It had all happened like this so often before, he implied.

Rachel packed feverishly, stuffing all her clothes into one case and several of the smaller packages into another. She would be glad of the opportunity of handing over the bracelets and two amber necklaces personally.

While she was pushing the last things in, Adrian went to get the car. She heard it hum into life beside the house, then it backed out on to the road.

She waited for Adrian to come in and help her with the heavy cases, but when he did not appear she bumped them down the stairs and out of the front door. Adrian was stooping under the bonnet of the car.

'What's the matter?'

His reply was inaudible but resentful. When he emerged there was a smear of grease across his forehead.

'The darned thing's just packed up on me. I can't make out what's wrong.'

The suspicion that he had deliberately contrived this crossed her mind; then she dismissed it. Adrian was unlikely to stoop to such methods to keep her here.

He said: 'I'll nip along to the shop and bring old Hans back with me. He's the expert.'

'Please hurry — I must get that plane.'

'I'll be right back.'

He hurried off along the road, and disappeared into the small red building beyond the church. Then there was silence but for the mournful cry of the swooping sea-birds and the rising wind.

Rachel felt the exasperation mounting in her throat. She was tempted to go back into the house and telephone for a car to come out along the wall. But it would take too long.

If Adrian took much longer she was going to miss her plane.

Suddenly, adding a new note to the sound of the wind, there came the unmistakable throb of another car. It grew louder as a large American car swung out from behind the end of the row of houses. It emerged on to the main road and came towards her, gathering speed. Then it slowed, its great chromium snout sliding in beside her.

The driver leaned out. It was the American who had spoken to her yesterday, outside the museum.

'Having trouble, lady?'

'The car won't work,' she explained

lamely. 'My . . . that is, someone's gone to fix it. To get someone to fix it.'

'You wouldn't be wanting a lift?'

'No, really, I . . . '

But there was no sign of Adrian. This man looked willing enough to help — and, according to her swift assessment, harmless enough.

'I'll be glad to be of assistance,' he urged her.

'Actually I want to get to the airport.'

'Schiphol? I guess I can manage that. I'm on my way to Rotterdam, so it fits in all right.'

Before she could waver any longer he got out and began to move her cases from one car to the other. Rachel looked along the road, wondering whether to ask him to drive her along to have a word with Adrian. The thought of the inevitable argument — time-wasting and irritating — restrained her. Adrian would undoubtedly disapprove of her accepting this lift.

She found a piece of paper in the glove compartment of Adrian's car, and scribbled him a note. She dropped it on the seat.

As they drove away along the dike, she

twisted round to look back. For as long as she could see the road in front of the houses there was still no sign of him. Then the curve of the wall took them round behind the town, and she settled back into her seat.

The car was heavy and fast. The road was new, there was no traffic. Rachel gave a little nod of satisfaction. They would make good time in this.

The driver said: 'Nice little bus, huh?'

'Very nice,' she agreed readily.

'My pride and joy, this.' He slowed as a group of workmen clambered up one side of the wall and crossed the road to the other. 'Oh, and say — maybe I ought to introduce myself. I'm Julius Kennedy.'

'It's good of you to help me, Mr Kennedy,' said Rachel. 'I'm Rachel . . . Petersen.' Always she heard herself making that little pause, like a catch in the breath, before she could utter her surname. It had never come naturally; never would. It was only some odd conventionality that prevented her from reverting to her maiden name. She still thought of herself as Rachel Watson. She had never been Mrs Petersen.

She wondered if she would be able to get used to being Mrs Adrian Brent.

Not that he's asked me, she thought. Not that he shows any immediate sign of asking. And not that I'm sure I want him to. Not yet. But later, not too much later, it will happen. And then . . . ?

She started, realizing that Julius Kennedy was speaking to her.

'Yes, sure, I know you're Mrs Petersen all right. We spoke yesterday, you recall.'

'Yes. I'm afraid I was a bit rushed at the time — '

'You must forgive me for intruding the way I did, but I wasn't figuring on having a lot of time in Stevinstad, and when I saw you I just automatically started talking.'

'You won't be going back there?'

'Can't say right now. Depends on the way business works out.'

'Business? I wouldn't have thought there was much business for anyone in Stevinstad. Ten years from now, perhaps.'

He nodded. He had a sombre, lean face, and his voice had a sagging, querulous drawl in it that matched his sardonic expression.

'That's so. No, my business is way up in the towns. The visit to Stevinstad was . . . well, I guess you would call it personal. Being close to it, I just had to hustle over and take a look at the place. It's kind of uncanny seeing a town — even the beginnings of a town — when you knew it only as water and some broken-up sandbanks.'

'You knew it before they started work on the dike?'

They were approaching land. That was how Rachel still thought of it: the polder and its wall and the town of Stevinstad were too new and impermanent, not yet safely established. Here the true land lay where it had lain for centuries.

Kennedy flipped his hand negligently towards the north.

'I was stationed way up there in the war,' he said. 'On the other side of the polder, where they started the new dike.'

'It must look very different now.'

'It sure does.' He slowed for a road junction, and the spire of a church jutted up from the plain ahead. Now traffic began to swish past. The sun came out, chasing the shadows of clouds across the fields. 'Nearly got drowned there once,' Kennedy reminisced, more to himself than to his passenger. 'The R.A.F. tried to blow a hole in one of the dikes while the Germans were still there. It didn't work, and they didn't try again — we got those guys on the run soon after that. But your boys had dented that dike more than anyone realized at the time. After the liberation — and after we were halfway across Germany — there were some of us sitting there when one hell of a storm blew up . . . and down went the wall.'

Rachel remembered hearing of this before. There were several people in Stevinstad who had been involved in that near-catastrophe, and some who had lost relatives.

'There wasn't a very heavy death roll,' she recalled.

'No. It wasn't a complete break, and they had it blocked up in pretty quick time. But the land up there was submerged for maybe a year. And a fine mess there was when they'd got the water out and started to rebuild!'

Rachel noticed suddenly that his chin was quivering. He reached in his pocket for a pack of cigarettes, and lit one single-handed, without offering her one. His mind was far away. His eyes were narrowed, and he looked as though he were in pain.

Then he was awake again. Once more he got the cigarettes out. This time he offered them to her.

'Sorry,' he said. 'Automatic, the way I light one for myself.'

They went some way in silence, and then he began to talk about her grandfather. He trotted out some of the banal questions they were so used to hearing, and Rachel answered without effort. Then she found that he was edging the conversation towards the topics he had mentioned at their brief meeting the previous day.

'You must have had a tough time clearing up all the things your grandfather left.'

'I kept fairly comprehensive records of

his findings,' said Rachel. 'And I've had plenty of help in classifying the material since he died.'

'Yes. That feller who was with you — or maybe he's a relative?'

Kennedy sounded casual, yet she felt that he was probing and would be keenly interested in her replies. She felt uneasy; but she could hardly refuse to give straight answers to innocuous questions.

She said: 'Adrian? He was a Deputy Keeper — you know — and then he got a two-year research fellowship. Now he's on a long leave, helping me.'

'He knows his stuff,' said Julius Kennedy idly.

'He does.'

Her grandfather, she knew, would not have said so. Hammond Watson had been asked to take Adrian along with him once or twice, and refused. 'Another of the booksy boys,' he had growled. She could still hear that derisive, uncompromising growl. 'Another damned public-school boy with all the right words and phrases pat on his tongue — and not an original idea in his head.'

This, at any rate, was a piece of information she need not offer gratuitously to Julius Kennedy.

'I'd sure like to see some of that collection,' he was saying. 'You've got it all organized now?'

'It should all be available to the public,' said Rachel rather pompously, 'within a year's time. Not all in one place, of course — '

'Now that's a pity.'

'The items in our house at Stevinstad will be moved by the day after tomorrow. Some will go to Amsterdam, and there are certain things that have been promised to Oslo and Copenhagen. Then there are some things in our home back in England — they'll be cleared within a few days of our getting back.'

The road led through a small town. Trees bent over the car from the pavements, and small gabled houses flickered behind hedges. An old clock tower stood at a crossroads. They were making good time. Rachel felt a rush of gratitude towards the American.

He said: 'With those big cases of yours,

118

I thought maybe you were shifting the whole lot by hand!'

She laughed. 'Only some of the smaller items. I'm on my way to Copenhagen.'

'That's a valuable load, then.'

'Not really.' She had explained this so many times to so many people. Again she heard her grandfather's rasping voice. He became even more furious than usual with questioners who took it for granted that some monetary value could be set on his findings. 'Some of our things,' Rachel said, 'are invaluable from the archaeological viewpoint. But they wouldn't fetch much actual cash.'

'You can't finance new projects by selling a few of the more precious items?'

'Hardly.'

They were out on the plain again. The fingers of a smooth lake prodded towards the edge of the road, and two white sails skimmed gently across the surface. The car hummed along a straight stretch that seemed to go on for ever, rising slightly over bridges and then settling down again. Kennedy's foot went down, but there was no sensation of increased speed.

'No chance of coming across anything . . . well, unexpected?' ventured Kennedy. 'There must be some things from the old days that are valuable in themselves — that you could raise money on.'

'To my grandfather,' said Rachel, 'things were only valuable if they proved something. Or,' she added wryly, 'if they disproved something.'

'Oh?' She was conscious of his slackening of interest, as though she were diverting the conversation from some line he had chosen. But then he said politely: 'What sort of things?'

'Well . . . bronze weapons that establish the date of a disinterred encampment, or runic stones that confirm the descent of kings and warriors. Fragments of cloth and the shape of ship graves, with their prows pointing towards England — all part of a picture that people like my grandfather built up in their minds until they were literally living in it.'

'You said something about disproving as well as proving.'

She remembered her grandfather's glee when he found some small shred of evidence that could be used against an enemy. Even the memory of his exultation made her feel uneasy. She began to wish she had not wandered off on to this topic.

She said: 'There were incidents like that over the Gribedyr.'

'What was that again?'

'The Gribedyr,' said Rachel. 'It was an animal that suddenly appeared in Nordic decorations. You found it everywhere. It didn't appear to develop from anything: it just appeared, and was taken up by everyone. It was in the form of a clutching beast.' Many a time she had had nightmares involving that weird creature. Then there had been absurdly pleasant dreams in which the animal had been pleasant and even cuddly. It had certainly haunted her at one period, when her grandfather was engaged in one of his bitter wars with the Danish archaeologist, Ascomann. 'The generally accepted theory,' she went on, 'was that it was developed by Nordic designers from their first impressions of a Frankish-Carolingian device — heraldic device, that is. It fascinated them, and they produced from it an odd mixture of lion, bear, dog, and goblin. The clutching beast . . . '

'Sounds pretty,' said Kennedy. 'But what was the argument? What did it prove, or not prove?'

'Ascomann, who never got on well with my grandfather, claimed that there were no Carolingian influences in the Gribedyr. He believed it was an absolutely pure Nordic product. He claimed that the Swedes had seen Caucasian bears in their travels through Russia, and invented the animal themselves. Once he dug up an armlet which he said proved this — and my grandfather proved it was a fake. Someone must have planted it there.'

'You mean — '

'We never knew,' said Rachel with a shudder. She could never forget the scandalous accusations and counter-accusations of those days. They had not been of much service to the reputation of international archaeology. 'There was a lot of dirt thrown around at the time. But it didn't settle. Or it didn't settle in any one place. My grandfather made a laughing stock of Ascomann; and Ascomann fired a lot of accusations at my grandfather. They said the disgrace of it killed Ascomann, because he knew that people suspected him of having produced a fake in an effort to prove one of his pet theories. My grandfather said that the thing he couldn't forgive him for was not producing a better fake!'

Kennedy shook his head in wonderment. 'They sure had fun, those boys. Seems crazy, getting so steamed up about things like that.'

There was something so disparaging in his voice that Rachel was jolted into recollection of their first meeting — recollection of an inconsistency. She said:

'But I thought you were interested in the subject?'

'Me? Oh, sure — '

'When I saw you outside the museum, you seemed terribly keen. You must have known what fanatics archaeologists are.'

'That's so. In fact, I — Say, this is the place where I've got to drop off and see some friends. Just a short stop while I go in and come out.'

They were entering a small, compact village. The name, Duurwijk, announced itself from a sign which stood at the entrance to a narrow street.

'Keep your elbows in!' Kennedy grinned.

The car bumped gently over the cobbles, between two rows of houses that crouched close to the ground. They had low windows and warped door-frames. Although the houses were packed together in long terraces, no two gables were alike. The wide American car had nosed into a mediaeval world.

'Here we are.'

Kennedy stopped outside a house with a green door, and cut the ignition. The sensation of having driven back into time was at once spoilt by the sound of a radio booming through an open window.

He got out, and came round to Rachel's side.

'Want to stretch your legs? I'll only be two or three minutes.'

Rachel got out into the narrow street. When Julius Kennedy had gone into the house, she sauntered along to the end of the street and found herself on a small bridge. A hundred yards away water was being pumped out of a lock, and a barge was moving slowly along the broad canal.

She turned back, suddenly impatient. If Kennedy came out again she wanted to be ready to leave immediately. But there was no sign of him. Nobody moved in the street.

Rachel walked slowly back, ready to quicken her pace if Kennedy appeared.

The car gave off a warm metallic smell. She was just about to get in again when the door of the house opened.

'Hold it.' It was Kennedy, leaning out. 'I'll be another five minutes or so. Plenty of time in hand. Would you care to come in and telephone your friend back in Stevinstad? Maybe he'd appreciate it.'

'Telephone?'

She could not help showing her surprise, and the American laughed.

'They do have a telephone in this old place,' he assured her. 'Come along in and see for yourself. I won't be long now — truly.'

He held the door open for her. Rachel went in. Instinctively she stooped. The ceiling was only a few inches above her head. If she had walked with too springy a step she would have banged her head on the beams.

The house was quiet, dark, cool, and smelling of damp. Kennedy seemed very much at home here. He guided her down a narrow passage to where a telephone jutted out from the wall — a telephone that was, she wanted to say out loud, even more mediaeval than the house itself or the street outside.

'I don't know how to operate this,' she protested. 'I know you crank the handle, but — '

'Let me fix it.'

He made the call for her. She could tell that his Dutch, though halting, was efficient. After a moment he held the receiver out to her.

'By the time you've finished, I'll be ready,' he promised.

She stood in the dank corridor, and heard Adrian's voice, tinny and remote.

'Rachel — what the devil are you up to?'

She explained. He kept interrupting her. He sounded unreasonably agitated.

'You don't know who this man is,' he

protested. 'Or what he is.'

'He's a perfectly ordinary, respectable American who was kind enough to offer me a lift,' said Rachel. 'And' — she could not resist the little jab — 'he's got a much faster car than ours, so I'll get there a lot sooner. I had enough of breathless take-offs with Grandad. This time I'll be able to *walk* to the plane.'

'But how can you tell that he's not . . . I mean, he might be in on it.'

'In on what?'

'Well, picking you up like that. Very smooth. He could be in on . . . on whatever that so-called Petersen is a part of. Unless . . . '

He stopped, but she could tell that he was still at the other end of the line. And she thought she could tell what he had been about to say. He was still wondering whether in fact the man who called himself Petersen really was Petersen — her husband.

Rachel said: 'Adrian, you're being very silly. It's nice of you to be so concerned about me, but truly, my dear, I'm all right. We'll be off in a minute. I'll ring you again from Copenhagen.'

In the hollow silence of the house she heard a familiar sound. It was a car engine murmuring into life.

Adrian was saying: 'I still think it'd be better if you — '

'Can't stop,' she broke in. 'We're ready to go. Give my love to Grandma.'

She slammed the receiver home just as the car revved up and moved away. She heard it go — and thought that it must be a different car. Then she realized that it couldn't be: there had been no room for another car in that street.

She gasped, and ran for the door. She reached it just as Julius Kennedy rushed out of a side door into the passage.

'What the hell . . . '

He almost knocked her against the wall as he dived for the front door and wrenched it open. A yell of fury broke from him. Staggering out into the street, he gaped incredulously after his car. It raced at a perilous speed over the cobbles, slid sideways as it reached the end of the street, and then was on the bridge. They heard the resonant sound of the bridge as it went over; and then it was gone.

Julius Kennedy grabbed Rachel's arm as though to hold himself up. His fingers bit into her flesh.

'Why, the goddam' thief . . . the . . . the . . . '

Abruptly he let go. With another snort of impotent anger he plunged back into the house.

6

Rachel felt guilty.

Julius Kennedy was treating the whole matter as a straightforward case of car stealing. He had been to the telephone and roared down it in Dutch that was even more spluttering than before, and now he was apologizing to her because she would miss her plane, and her cases were in his car, and if he could get his hands on that son of a bitch . . .

Rachel felt that she was the one who ought to do the apologizing. But she could hardly do that without telling him the full story of yesterday's incredible happenings; and she was not prepared to let a stranger in on that bewildering story. Yet surely this theft was part of the same story? It wasn't an ordinary theft: it couldn't be; that was too much of a coincidence.

Somebody wanted to stop her going to Denmark. Or at any rate postpone her trip. Or else they wanted to go through her cases, driven away in the car.

Or to get hold of her papers — her passport, her marriage certificate . . . That seemed crazy, but in the context of yesterday's events it was not so crazy. The pattern made no sense yet, but there *was* a pattern.

The man who called himself Petersen — had he really left on that plane this morning? And if not, how had he known she would be here? Had they been followed?

Nobody could have guessed that the car would break down, that this American would pick her up and drive her along this route.

Unless Kennedy himself were mixed up in it, as Adrian had said over the phone.

Or Adrian himself, she thought wildly. He might have chased them, or telephoned somebody, working out their probable route; or . . .

No. She had to stop her mind going round in these futile circles. Too many pieces of the jigsaw were missing. And she had a desperate feeling that she was losing pieces rather than finding them.

Trying to collect herself, she said: 'I must ring Stevinstad. I'll get Adrian to come and pick me up.'

'I can order a car,' said Kennedy. 'There's nothing in this little dump, but we're only five miles from — '

'Thank you,' said Rachel, 'but you've done enough. I must let Adrian know what has happened, and then I suppose I'll have to go back to Stevinstad with him — or to Amsterdam, to get myself a new passport. Otherwise I'll never be able to get back to England!'

Kennedy whistled. 'Your passport was in that lot? Say, that's tough. I wish I hadn't stopped off here. This is the last place you'd expect car thieves to operate. It beats me.'

She asked him to make the call for her, and a minute later she was once more speaking to Adrian in Stevinstad. His first explosion of alarm gave way to a justifiable tone of 'I told you so'. He did not actually utter those words, but they lurked behind everything he said, and Rachel could hardly resent them. In any case, she felt warmed by his immediate response: of course he would come and fetch her at once. The car was in running order again; he would leave in less than five minutes' time.

She wanted very much to see him. He was a known, reliable point of reference in a world that seemed to be growing more and more irrational.

While they waited for him to arrive, Julius Kennedy took her into the tiny sitting-room from which he had emerged with such fury when his car raced away. It was square and very white, with an uneven tiled floor. An old clock ticked on the wall, its pendulum swinging drowsily over the table in the corner. A middle-aged woman with a plump face was sitting at the table. Her features were Dutch enough, but she had none of the characteristic pink good health of most people round here: she was pale and flabby, as though she spent too much time indoors, and her eyes were sullen. Introducing her to Rachel, Kennedy referred to her merely as Sophie. The introduction was no more than a grudging formality. After that, he and Sophie exchanged only a few words. The three of them sat and waited. At the end of fifteen minutes Sophie got up and went out silently, to return in due course with a pot of coffee and three cups.

Rachel tried to make conversation about the house and the town, using Kennedy as interpreter, but it petered out. She had the impression that Kennedy was not translating adequately, either because he could not or did not wish to.

Adrian seemed to take a lifetime in coming. She had nearly given up hope when at last the sound of the car resonated between the cramped walls of the street.

Rachel was first out of the house. She was on the pavement as Adrian slammed the door of the car.

'So you're all right,' he said. It was not so much an expression of relief as an intimation that she hardly deserved to be safe.

'Adrian, I'm so glad to see you. I was really beginning to feel that anything melodramatic was liable to happen.'

'I told you over the phone that you

oughtn't to have cleared off with that American. If you'd listened to me — '

'By the time you were lecturing me on that point,' Rachel reminded him, 'the thief must already have been getting into the car. It was driven off while you were talking.'

'The whole thing seems pretty fishy to me.' Adrian, she sensed, was even more agitated than he had sounded on the phone. He looked badly shaken, and kept glancing apprehensively over her shoulder, through the open doorway behind her. 'I don't like it. If you ask me, this benefactor of yours — '

He broke off. Rachel turned. Julius Kennedy was hurrying out of the house.

He said: 'They've found it!'

'Oh, I'm so glad.'

'I've just had the call — just as I was following you out.'

'Where is the car?'

'Only five miles from here. It was found abandoned by the roadside, close by a clump of bushes. No damage done, so they tell me. But from what I can make out, your cases have been opened.

Maybe' — he looked anxious to reassure her — 'the thief hasn't taken anything too important.'

Rachel grimaced. 'There wasn't anything important to take. As long as my passport is still there, that'll be something.'

Adrian said curtly: 'When will they be bringing the car back?'

Kennedy gave him a nod of welcome. 'They're still examining it. They say if I care to get myself out there to drive it back, they'll probably be finished by the time I get there.' He flickered a meaning glance at the blue Consul that waited on the cobbles.

'But of course,' said Rachel at once. 'You must come out with us. You can collect your car, and we can collect my luggage. It's the obvious thing to do.'

'There's certainly something in that,' Kennedy agreed gratefully. 'If you're sure it wouldn't be too much trouble — '

'None at all.' Rachel was firm.

Adrian frowned. But all he said was, uneasily: 'As long as we don't run into any ambush . . . or anything.'

'What kind of ambush do you have in mind, sir?' asked Kennedy.

'Oh, I don't know.'

'Don't let's allow our imaginations to run away with us,' said Rachel hastily. 'Shall we go?' Then she hesitated, glancing back at the house. 'I must just run in and say — '

'Don't worry about Sophie,' said Kennedy. 'I'll tell her all about it when we get back. When I get back, that is. I'll say your goodbyes for you, shall I?'

They drove off, over that same bridge over which the larger car had throbbed earlier in the day. The landscape opened up again, with the road laid down ahead of them like a ruler.

Adrian said: 'You know the way to this place?'

'I know it all right. Keep straight on until we hit the first junction, then I'll direct you from there.'

Kennedy was sitting in the back seat, while Rachel and Adrian were in front. Adrian was bristling. He might have been afraid that the man in the back was about to thrust a gun between his shoulders. He drove hard and tensely, without his usual relaxation.

They approached a crossroads, and Adrian slowed.

'To the right,' said Kennedy. They swung to the right, and then he said: 'Take the left fork there, and keep going. I figure it must be a mile along that way.'

There were trees on both sides of the road now, flickering past. Rachel tried to follow them with her eyes, until there was an ache of protest in her eye muscles.

'There!' snapped Kennedy abruptly.

His car was tilted away from the road, half-hidden behind a small cluster of bushes. They swung in close, and Adrian cut his engine. When they got out, there was silence apart from the singing of the telegraph wires like an electric kettle boiling away overhead.

A man emerged from behind the bushes. He was in police uniform, and moved heavily and imposingly. He saluted, and began to talk to Adrian in Dutch.

Adrian waved desperately towards Julius Kennedy.

Kennedy launched once more into a

language that with him managed to be simultaneously nasal and guttural. The policeman nodded, and after a moment indicated that they should go and examine the car.

Glancing back as they went, followed at a distance by Rachel and Adrian, Kennedy said: 'His buddies have gone off with some photographs and prints to the town so they can put out the dogs right away. They'll question everyone in the neighbourhood — and in these parts of Holland, where everyone watches every-one else as a matter of course, they ought to get on his trail without any trouble.' He inspected the car; walked right round it; peered inside. 'Not that I care so much, now that I've got the automobile back. So long as it's sound, that's all I ask.' Then he went on hurriedly: 'But your things, Mrs Petersen — you must be thinking I'm pretty selfish to go on like this. Why not get in and check through your cases?'

He had a brief interchange with the policeman, who nodded and opened the door so that Rachel could get in.

The thief had evidently driven the car

off the road and then settled in the back seat to go through her belongings. Unless he had had an accomplice who had carried out the search while they were driving along. The cases had been propped across the seat and opened, and the contents had been shaken out over the seat and the floor. Rachel began to pick things up, one at a time.

She soon found her handbag under the pile. The passport was there, intact. So were her travellers' cheques — no good to anyone, anyway, she supposed; and if they *had* been stolen by someone confident of being able to forge her signature, she had at any rate a record of the numbers and could have done something about it. The cash that had been in her bag was gone; but there had been very little of it.

'Well?' Adrian's head came down beside the window.

'I'm still checking.' She quickly pushed some of her more attractive underwear, now a trifle rumpled, into the case, and came to some torn brown paper and cardboard. 'They've taken this, though. Or he has, if there was just one man.'

Adrian recognized the wrappings immediately. That was hardly to be wondered at, for he had worked with her on the classifying and packing of the various items from her grandfather's hoard.

He said: 'Which would that be? One of the bracelets?'

'I'll have to get them all together.'

It was clear that all her clothes were still here. There was nothing of value among her personal belongings. But all the small packages for Copenhagen had been opened. Three items were missing; the others lay on the floor or the seat. The three missing treasures were two bracelets and a necklace.

Rachel got out of the car. The policeman and Julius Kennedy stood waiting enquiringly.

Rachel said to Kennedy: 'Tell him, will you, that a small amount of money has been stolen — it couldn't have been more than fifty guilders — and that two old Danish bracelets and a necklace have gone, too.'

'I thought you said they weren't valuable?' Kennedy probed.

'Archaeologically you can think of them as real treasure,' said Rachel. 'From any other point of view, they aren't of much value. Not worth robbing a car for, anyway. I don't think there's any market for stolen grave ornaments.'

Kennedy studied her dubiously for a moment, then turned to the policeman and began to translate. The policeman stopped him after a moment or two.

Kennedy said: 'He'd like a detailed description of the items you can be sure were stolen.'

Adrian fidgeted. 'Couldn't we drive into the town and do all that sort of thing at the police station?'

'But we don't want to go in that direction,' said Rachel quickly. 'The route to the airport is over that way, surely?'

Adrian nearly exploded. 'You don't mean to say you're still thinking — '

'I've missed the plane for which I had a booking,' said Rachel. 'But there'll be another. We must contact van Eck — his man at the airport will be going crazy by now.'

'You can't go ahead now,' Adrian

protested. 'We've got to talk — try to sort this out . . . '

He became aware that she was frowning a warning at him, and he quietened down. Kennedy, who had been following the outburst with frank interest, coughed and tried to pretend that he had been sunk in a reverie.

It took time to give a full description of the bracelets and necklace, particularly through an interpreter who found difficulty in translating some of the more technical terms. But in the end it was down. And then there were other problems. Adrian took a lot of persuading. Once out of earshot of Kennedy, the two of them argued. Adrian, at the wheel of the Consul, said that he was going to drive back to Stevinstad. Rachel said they were going to proceed to Schiphol. Adrian said they were not. Rachel said that she had no intention, now, of giving up — and she meant it. She did not understand why anyone should wish to steal those ornaments from her luggage, but she was going to find out. She did not understand how they tied up with the behaviour of the tall Dane yesterday, but that, too, she was going to find out. They were not going to stop her; and Adrian was not going to frighten her off.

'It's sheer madness to go on,' said Adrian.

'I'm not going back.'

'You don't know what you're getting into.'

'I shan't rest until I've got into it,' said Rachel; 'and out of it again.'

He gave in, as she had known he would. She had known it because she was determined to go on, and it was inconceivable that she should not get her own way in this. At the same time, once he had acknowledged defeat and turned the car towards the distant airport, she felt an odd little tremor of disillusionment. Had she wanted him to dominate her? It was absurd. Yet she half-longed for Adrian to take matters into his own hands. If he had told her what to do and stuck to it instead of arguing with her, she would have been furious for a time; but after that she would have felt a bit . . . well, smug. She wanted to experience that sensation. Even if she hated it, she wanted to know what it was like.

Van Eck himself was at Schiphol. He was in quite a state. He had been telephoning, trying without success to get in touch with her. When she presented him with her demands for revised arrangements for a flight to Copenhagen, he did not know whether to be relieved or infuriated.

While they waited for van Eck to book what seat he could, Adrian had a last attempt.

'It would be much better for you to come back to Stevinstad,' he said. 'It'll save an awful lot of trouble if we get the place cleared up and all three of us go back to England together. All this wandering off to Denmark and then back to England on your own — I'm sure something will get overlooked.'

'You've been efficient enough so far,' Rachel flattered him. 'I'm quite sure everything will go all right.'

'I'll be glad when it's all over.'

'So will I,' said Rachel. 'Then we can . . . settle down.'

As soon as she had said it, she felt herself going pink. Fortunately Adrian did not read anything into the words. He simply said:

'I still think you ought to call this silly business off. It's bound to lead to trouble. More trouble than you think, perhaps.'

'But what kind of trouble?' demanded Rachel. She did not want to admit how apprehensive she felt now that the time for departure was drawing closer. 'Nothing violent can happen.'

'I wouldn't be too sure.' Oddly, she thought, he did not sound so much concerned with her welfare as with establishing the fact that he had warned her — so that, later, he could once more have that 'I told you so' note in his voice.

'As long as you get Grandma through the Customs all right,' she laughed, 'there's nothing else to worry about.'

'As long as I get what?' It came snapping back at her with unexpected force.

'I said as long as you get Grandma through the Customs . . . ' She shook her head. 'What's wrong? It was only a facetious remark.'

'Seems rather pointless.'

'Adrian, there's no need to sound so cross.'

'I'm sorry. It's just that I like things to be neat and orderly. I'd much sooner you were coming back with me.'

Rachel sighed. 'So you've told me, in various ways. But I'm not going to come, Adrian. Not until I've got my past straightened out and settled in my own mind, once and for all. It should only take a few days. And then . . . '

And then what? She could not look that far ahead. So far she had given little thought to the future. Her grandfather had established an exclusive claim on her life for so long that the mere idea of being on her own produced a swirl of vertigo. There were decisions to be made, but she was not ready for them yet. Even during these months since his death, she had still been engrossed in Hammond Watson's affairs. Now the end was in sight; and so was the end of her own brief, disconcerting experience of two men calling themselves Erik Petersen. Beyond that, nothing was visible.

Van Eck came back. He held out a small paper wallet towards her as though offering a challenge.

'You will leave' — it was both an order and a prayer — 'at six o'clock. It will be necessary to spend the night in Copenhagen. There is a train from Copenhagen at nine o'clock tomorrow morning, which connects with the Hennesø ferry from the west coast of Zealand.'

'It's so good of you, Mr van Eck,' breathed Rachel. 'I don't know where I'd be without you. When I think of all you've done for me over the years . . .'

It was like exposing a pink and white ice-cream to the rays of the sun. Van Eck's grumpiness sagged; the pink ran into the white; he made little sploshy deprecating noises, and when Rachel shook hands with him he clasped both his hands round hers.

'You will not be leaving us for ever?' he implored her. 'You will come back to Holland?'

She had no idea whether she would be coming back; no idea of her life next week, next month, or next year. But she said: 'I'm sure I shall be back, Mr van Eck. Back to trouble you!'

'It is no trouble. It will never be trouble.'

There was time for a drink, and then at last she was on the plane. Adrian and his arguments fell away below. The flat land of Holland turned slowly beneath the plane, then settled. Above a light film of cloud there was dazzling sunshine.

At Copenhagen everything was smooth and efficient and unexpectedly uneventful. Rachel had half-anticipated some melodramatic incident. She was surprised that her luggage had not gone astray, that the plane had not been shot down, that the airport bus did not circle Copenhagen and dash away into the country with her. In her hotel room there was nobody lurking in the wardrobe, and when she picked up the phone to call one of her grandfather's old friends, there was no sinister laughter on the line.

She arranged to deliver the grave ornaments she had brought with her — those that remained after the robbery

— and also gave Professor Hansen the details of four items that she had had to leave with the Customs for clearance. His well-remembered voice, silky and respectful, made her feel at ease even over the phone. Before the conversation was ended he had persuaded her that she must come to have dinner with himself and his family, and twenty minutes later there was a cab outside waiting for her.

As she stepped into it, Rachel was suddenly reminded of scenes in films where cabs drove madly away. You ought never, she recalled, to take the first cab, and certainly not one that claimed to be waiting for you. She should have summoned another one.

It was almost an anticlimax when she found herself being delivered safely to Professor Hansen's door.

The atmosphere was so mellow that evening, the hospitality so soothing and reassuring, that the thought of tomorrow receded. When she went back to her hotel that night she found it impossible to believe that she would find anything exciting on Hennesø. She would simply make a trip by train and boat, she would be met by an ordinary, everyday explanation of the recent events, and then she would go contentedly back to England and that would be that.

In the morning, on the train, she knew that this was ridiculous. Whatever the explanation might be, it could hardly be an ordinary one.

She wanted to urge the train on; and, a few hours later, to drive the boat more swiftly across the smooth dazzling waters of the Kattegat. Hennesø was visible for at least an hour before they seemed to make any progress towards it. Then, in the last fifteen minutes, it was dragged towards them across the ripples, the red-washed houses and the white chimneys of the herring smoke-houses taking on sharper outlines as the gap closed.

It was late afternoon when Rachel set foot on the island.

7

There were small boats with white hulls and green sails at the quayside. Fishing nets were stretched in the sun to dry, draped from the masts of the boats or from a length of line on the quay. The houses clustered close to the water's edge in a huddle of red and white. They were like a stage set: you sensed that there was nothing behind them — no streets, no further buildings; only the gently undulating fields.

Rachel asked the way to Hvidfelt. The fisherman she had spoken to did not understand English. Neither did the next one. She saw people turning to look at her. Two women came hospitably towards her, chattering happily together. One of them nodded when she mentioned Hvidfelt, and signalled to a man sitting on a bollard. He got up reluctantly, but his smile was friendly enough.

None of them spoke English, but the

name of Hvidfelt was enough. They conferred, pointed several times up the road leading out of the village, and then the man waved and a car appeared as though in answer to an incantation.

Rachel had left the larger of her two cases in Copenhagen. She pushed the one she had brought with her on to the back seat, and got in the front.

'English?' said the driver with a welcoming, approving grin.

'Yes,' said Rachel.

'Hvidfelt?'

'Yes, please.'

That was all that the driver had to offer. He put his foot down, and they moved away from the houses. The slope rose slightly, and a minute later Rachel saw the sea to their right, burnished more brightly than the shield that had hung on her grandfather's wall. It was obscured by a long, low farmhouse, then came into view again. The tilt of a field would hide it; then the burning mirror would return. Burial mounds were dark and hunched against the glare.

The journey took ten minutes, and

ended in a clean, scrubbed farmyard. The farmhouse was white, newly painted, with a red roof. Two men coming from one of the outbuildings waved to the driver, but did not come across to the car.

Rachel held out a handful of coins from the change she had collected at her hotel. The driver selected what he required, nodded stiffly, and said: '*Tusind tak.*' Then he gestured towards the door of the farmhouse, and towards her case, and raised his eyebrows.

'No, thank you,' she said automatically.

He smiled, got back into the car, and backed out into the narrow dusty road.

There was no reason why she should not have let him carry her case to the door and knock. But somehow she wanted him to leave. She wanted, she thought wryly, to have her retreat cut off, so that she could only go forward.

She picked up the case and carried it up to the door. There was no sound from inside the house. At the back of the building a man was calling something in a heavy, unhurried way. The stutter of the car's engine faded away down the road.

Rachel lifted her hand, and knocked on the door.

All the breath at once seemed to go out of her. She fully expected the man who called himself Erik Petersen to open the door — and she was sure he would be smiling, having expected her all along, being prepared for her. She was walking into a trap. He had set it, and here she was.

The door opened. Framed in the opening was an elderly man with unflawed silver hair and pale blue eyes.

He half-bowed, and said: '*Goddag?*' There was a lilt of enquiry in it.

'You are Hr Petersen?'

'*Jo.*'

'I am Rachel Petersen.' This time she brought out the surname defiantly, without the usual hesitation.

He stared. His mouth worked, but he said nothing. Rachel was suddenly very much alone. It was possible that her impulsive chase had ended at the doorway of an old man who spoke no English and could offer her no help at all; or who still hated the son who had refused to have anything to do with him, and so might well pretend not to know a word of English anyway.

Then Petersen reached down and picked up her case from the step.

'You will come in?' The words were thick and awkward, carefully turned over before being uttered.

'I am Erik's wife,' said Rachel distinctly, so that there should be no misunderstanding. 'Or rather' — how could she have put it so clumsily? — 'his widow.'

They stopped in the whitewashed passage, in a shaft of sunlight striking across from an open door. Petersen looked at her, blinking slightly. He looked worried; whether by what she had said or by the need to phrase a reply, it was difficult to tell. Evidently he had to stand still while he thought things out, and pulled them into shape.

At last he said: 'But Erik is not dead. And you are not his wife.'

Before she could say any more, he had led the way into the sunlit room beyond.

The shadows were long. The sun was only just above the crown of the gently sloping hill outside. It struck flashes of brightness from the glass over innumerable photographs, hanging from the walls and propped on the mantelpiece.

In the window sat a woman of Petersen's age. She turned her grey head towards Rachel. Petersen spoke to her in Danish, and Rachel heard the woman catch her breath and say something that sounded both pitying and disbelieving.

'You will sit down?' tried Petersen.

Rachel took a chair close to the window so that she could see the woman full face. As she did so, the sun slid down behind the hill. The light in the room was diffused. A few scattered rays stabbed in, and then the brightness had gone.

Petersen came and stood beside his wife. The formal introduction was unnecessary. You could tell they were man and wife: together in the room, they could not have been envisaged apart. And whatever the truth about Erik Petersen might be, one thing was certain: if he felt any hostility towards his parents, the fault was his own; there was an essential sweetness in their features that could be sensed without either of them having to speak.

Rachel said: 'I've come here because I want to find out the truth about my husband.'

The two of them conferred silently. Then the man ventured: 'You write a letter to us.'

'I write . . . ? Oh, oh yes. I wrote to you when he died. Then you *did* get it. But you didn't reply.'

There was another long pause. It was possible to feel the man's groping for a coherent sentence almost as a physical effort.

'My son says he will reply. Said he will reply. You did not get a letter?'

'Not a word,' said Rachel.

Petersen shook his head. His wife muttered something. He shook his head again, and then held out his hands pleadingly towards Rachel.

'Please . . . '

He was asking for time. She sat there, wishing she could help him to assemble the words he needed. He was such a nice old man, and the struggle was painful to watch.

At last he put his head back bravely.

'Please,' he said again. 'We receive your letter. It is hard to read. At first we do not understand. It says that our son is dead and that you are his wife. But we see him two days ago, and he is not married. When he comes back, we . . . we ask. We say what is this? Then he tells us.'

Rachel gripped the arms of her chair. Here it came! Would his halting English be good enough to make the story clear?

He took a deep breath and floundered on. 'Weeks ago he is robbed. In Copenhagen. He works there then, he is robbed. First he finds it is his money. Then later he finds . . . no passport. And there are other papers. He tells the police, but they find nothing.'

For some reason a question forced itself to Rachel's lips. 'He did tell the police?' She could not explain the doubt that had prompted this.

Old Petersen nodded vigorously. 'He tells the police. His passport, money, many papers. But Flemming is not going abroad, so — '

'Flemming?'

'Our son.'

'But I'm talking about Erik.'

'He is Erik Flemming Petersen. Always we call him Flemming. I am Erik also.'

'Please go on,' said Rachel.

'When he wishes a new passport, he asks, and tells them about the robbery. There are enquiries. He gets a new passport.'

'But the man I married — '

'You are not the wife of my son,' said the old man, distressed at having to say this. 'The man who steals Flemming's papers — that is who married you. And he is dead?'

'He's dead,' said Rachel.

'And you write to us . . . ' He looked pitifully at his wife, who recognized her cue to smile sadly and sympathetically at Rachel. 'When we get your letter, we wait for Flemming to come home, and we ask him what it is. And' — he frowned — 'he says he writes to you to explain. He tells us we must not worry, he will write.'

It solved nothing. Why should anyone who had stolen another man's passport and personal documents get married under a false name? Why? . . .

You only had to start asking questions to see why this story would not hang together.

Rachel said: 'I never got any letter. I don't believe one was ever written. What I *did* get . . . '

Her voice petered out. Old Petersen was leaning towards her, straining to understand every word. And if he did understand, what would he make of it? Whatever the plot might be, the old man was not involved in it. He had been telling the truth: Rachel had no doubt whatever in her mind about this. His son Flemming — and she had no doubt that this was the mocking, incredible man who had appeared so fantastically at Stevinstad the day before yesterday — had said that he would write to the poor misguided widow who had announced his 'death'; and Flemming had not done so. Flemming had done nothing at all . . . until the day when the monument was unveiled; and then he had shown up in Stevinstad, pretending to be her husband.

Which meant that he must have known

the man who had really married her.

Should she tell this old man that fact? Should she take him over the story, step by step? If his son's passport and papers had been stolen, how did that son come to know so much about her life with the man she had married?

She looked at that puzzled, worried face, and knew that she could not bring herself to do it. He was not to blame in this. He wanted enlightenment as much as she did. But it might hurt him if he received it.

She said: 'Where is . . . your son?'

'He is in Copenhagen.'

'Oh no.'

He raised his hand eagerly, asking her to wait. 'No. He is in Copenhagen yesterday. Today he is here. He goes to see a friend. He comes back ten minutes. Half-hour, maybe.'

His wife got up and turned towards the door that undoubtedly led to the kitchen.

In moving, she revealed a photograph that had so far been obscured by her head. Rachel had been only dimly conscious of the innumerable faces looking out of the other pictures that hung in congested disarray all over the walls, but this one sprang into focus at once. It was more recent than the others, many of which were yellowed with age, and the outlines were more clearly defined.

Old Petersen was trying to say something, but she did not hear him. The faces of the two young men in the photograph looked out at her, and drew her towards them. She got up, and took three steps forward.

Two faces. One of them that of the man she now knew must be old Petersen's son. The other that of her dead husband.

Petersen shuffled up behind her. She spun round.

'That is Erik!' she cried.

He nodded. 'Erik.'

'But you said — I mean . . . '

'Erik,' he said, 'and my son Flemming.'

Rachel put out a hand to catch the back of the nearby chair and steady herself.

She said: 'Who is the Erik in the picture?'

'He is my wife's . . . you call it . . . nephew?'

'Yes, nephew. And your son's cousin, then.'

'That is what you say? Yes, so I have heard it. A cousin. They are alike, yes?'

'In many ways,' said Rachel grimly.

'A great man, his father.'

'Who was he?'

'Hans Ascomann. You have heard of him — the great . . . great . . . '

He could not find the word. He didn't need to. As far as Rachel was concerned there could be only one Hans Ascomann. Her grandfather's enemy, the man derided and made a fool of by Hammond Watson!

She heard the whisper rasp in her mouth: 'And this . . . '

'Erik Ascomann,' nodded old Petersen. 'Erik, the son of our great Hans.'

8

'I suppose,' said Erik Flemming Petersen, 'that I must give you an explanation.'

'I think you owe me one,' said Rachel.

He had come into the room just when she felt that she could wait no longer. The atmosphere had been intolerable. The concern of the old couple had been upsetting. They were distressed that she had not been told what they considered to be the truth, and without telling them the full story so far — which would brand their son a liar — she could not discuss the matter any further. She was glad to see the son when he came; glad, and at the same time bitter with anger against him.

He glanced at his parents. They looked from him to Rachel and back again. Their obvious affection for him was returned: Rachel could see that in his reassuring smile.

Old Petersen said something. The

younger man interrupted him in a warm, comforting tone. Then he turned to Rachel.

'Perhaps you will come and see what it is like — the outside? It will be easier.'

'I can imagine that,' said Rachel tersely.

He led her out of the house. They went down a flagged path beside the main building, and crossed a yard to where the fields began. Ahead was the crown of the hill she had seen from the window. To the right, the grass sloped down gently to an inlet where the water was dark, in shadow. There was no shore: the grass ran right down into the creek.

A mile beyond, there was a bright splash of red buildings on a headland. A tall chimney thrust up into the evening sky. The red did not spoil the beauty of the coastline, but added a gay blob of colour to it.

'The canning factory,' explained the man beside her, following the direction of her gaze.

'Yes.'

He slowed his pace, and indicated a seat that had been placed below a clump of beech trees, looking down on the water.

'I don't want to sit down,' said Rachel. 'I don't think I could.'

She wanted to walk furiously, to keep moving. She needed to drive energy up into her mind so that she could attack him and keep him on the run. She did not want to relax: she was not going to be soothed by the evening into accepting the sort of glib lies he had told his mother and father.

He shrugged and smiled. It was an agreeable smile, but a nervous one. All right, thought Rachel; let him be nervous. He had good cause to be.

They paced along the grassy verge of the water. The sun had gone well down below the hill, and a cool breeze came up off the inlet. Out in the open Kattegat there were still streaks of dazzling gold, but here the shadows crept up and took possession of the island.

He said: 'You know now that I am Erik Flemming Petersen.'

'Yes.'

'My family call me Flemming. When

. . . when Erik took my name for a time, he preferred to announce himself to you as Erik. It was more natural to him, of course, since he was really Erik.'

Rachel said crisply: 'The main thing, as far as I'm concerned, is why he took your name — and married me under that name.'

'Because you would have recognized his real name.'

'I don't see what could possibly — '

'Your grandfather,' said Flemming Petersen, 'would certainly not have allowed anyone with the name of Ascomann inside his house, would he?'

'Certainly not.'

'It is not a common name. He would at once have thought of his old enemy.'

'Naturally.'

'And Erik Ascomann would not have been able to get near him.'

'But why,' demanded Rachel, 'should he *want* to get near my grandfather? Why should he want to get into the house?'

Flemming Petersen tried to sound casual, but did not succeed. He said: 'He wanted to find the Gribedyr armlet.'

Rachel stiffened. 'Which one? We found quite a few at one time and another. Several of them were distributed to museums.'

But somehow she knew what he was going to say. It still did not make sense, but she had an intuitive glimmering of what direction the explanation was going to take.

He said: 'Not the Rus one.'

He was luring her on. He was hoping she would stumble and make some admission. But what admission? She had none to make.

She said: 'There never was a Rus one. That was Ascomann's theory, not my grandfather's. There was only a fake Rus armlet. I'm sure you know all this perfectly well.'

'Old Ascomann thought otherwise. He had to admit that the one he had unearthed was a fake; but that didn't mean that real ones didn't exist. He was convinced, until the day he died, that the fake was planted in the ground for him to find by Hammond Watson.'

Rachel stopped. He automatically went on a couple of steps, then turned to face her. His eyes were challenging yet troubled.

She snapped: 'That's absolute non-sense. It's slanderous. Do you think a man of my grandfather's standing would do a thing like that? It would be against all his beliefs.'

She said it proudly and confidently, but a vicious little doubt prickled uneasily in her mind. She knew it hadn't happened like that; but had she the right to be so dogmatic about the possibility itself? She remembered her grandfather's malice, his childish spite, his unquenchable desire to score off his enemies.

And Flemming Petersen was saying: 'I think of your grandfather as an iconoclast rather than a believer. He loved to smash other people's beliefs.'

It was true, but she felt a surge of defensive anger.

'He had no patience with gullible old men,' she said. 'Pedants who persisted in clinging to pet theories, deceiving them-selves and everyone else — he had no time for them. He considered it his duty to smack them down.'

'He enjoyed himself doing so.'

Rachel said: 'This still doesn't amount to an explanation. Nothing like it.'

'It is all a part of it,' he assured her. 'Old Ascomann had to admit that the armlet he had discovered was a fake. The arguments put forward by Hammond Watson when it was shown to him were sound ones. But the proof was not in the inscriptions or in the figure of the clutching beast itself, or in the cage motif around it. Those all fitted in exactly with what Ascomann was looking for — what he had been looking for over many years . . . '

'And because he was looking for them,' Rachel took him up, echoing her grandfather's contemptuous criticism, 'he swallowed the whole thing as authentic. It was my grandfather who had to point out that the bronze was of recent origin, so that the armlet could not be genuine.'

'But somewhere,' said Flemming Petersen quietly, 'there *was* a genuine armlet.'

He began to walk again, looking out across the darkening water. Rachel hurried to catch him up.

'What on earth are you talking about?'

'It was Ascomann's belief that the decoration on that armlet could only have been copied from a genuine original. He was confident that the real thing must exist somewhere.'

'A stubborn old fool,' said Rachel, 'clinging to a discredited theory. *Willing* himself to go on believing it.'

'That may be true,' conceded Petersen. 'I can assure you that he did believe. I didn't have a lot to do with my uncle, but on the few occasions when I saw him towards the end of his life I know he was obsessed with this idea. Your grandfather had visited the site. He could have planted the fake there for my uncle to find.'

'He could have done,' said Rachel scornfully; 'but he didn't.'

'The fact is that Ascomann believed that this is what happened. He died believing it. And after his death, his son Erik — my cousin — went on believing.'

There was a silence. Rachel shivered. It was not just the chill of the evening that gripped her. She remembered Erik. She remembered his bitterness and the tight hostility of his mouth and the bleak fanaticism that she had always sensed within him. The son of Hans Ascomann could hardly have been other than a fanatic!

'To think of a son inheriting a father's wild obsession . . . ' She shivered again.

He went on: 'The two of them had always been devoted. Erik's mother died when he was young. There were no other children, and he and his father were very close. He was my cousin, but I did not see him often. Not until after his father's death, that is. They were always together. Too much together, my mother used to say. It was not good. Not good for Erik, that I am sure. But there it was. When my Uncle Hans died — and you know, I think of him as the great Ascomann, one of our great figures, rather than as my own uncle — when he died, Erik was very alone. He thought too much. And one day, a long time after his father's death, a young man came to see him. It was a young man who had worked for Hammond Watson. Your grandfather had dismissed him.'

'He did that to plenty of young men,'

observed Rachel. 'Very few stayed for more than a few months.'

'This one was dismissed for dishonesty.'

'There were plenty of those.'

'He was angry. He hated your grandfather. He was a young Dane, and he was proud of his knowledge of our country's history. Your grandfather made his life unpleasant, laughed at him — and in the end threw him out. So he came to Erik Ascomann to tell him something.'

'To get his own back.'

'Of course. He was perhaps not a pleasant young man. But he appeared to be telling the truth. While he was with your grandfather, he examined some things he ought not to have seen — '

'On one of his pilfering bouts?' flashed Rachel. 'Probably the sort of thing for which he was fired.'

'It may be. But he claimed to have found an armlet. He knew of the controversy, and he recognized the armlet as matching the description originally given by Ascomann. He did not have time to examine it in detail — but his impression was that it was a genuine Rus armlet.'

'But there never was any such thing — it was a mistaken theory!'

'Was it? Not according to Ascomann; and not according to his son Erik. The young man who was dismissed said that the workmanship seemed crude; but that would fit in with it being an original one — one of those from which the Gribedyr derived. It could have been' — he spoke heavily and earnestly — 'the original on which Hammond Watson based his forgery.'

Rachel said: 'There was no such original. I would have known if there had been. My grandfather would not have been able to keep it to himself, even if he had wanted to.'

Flemming Petersen shrugged. 'That may be so. What we are dealing with are the things that Erik and his father *believed*. When Erik heard this story, there was at once only one idea in his mind. His father had died of a broken heart because of your grandfather's attack on him. Erik had loved his father with a quiet passionate devotion. Now he learnt — or seemed to learn — that your grandfather had deliberately withheld a discovery that would have proved Hans Ascomann's theories to be true. He had to see that proof: he had to get his hands on it and show it to the world.

'I did not hear about his first steps until a year after he had started. During that year he persuaded several young men — friends and colleagues of his — to seek employment with your grandfather. Some of them were turned away, but two of them worked with him for a week or two, and another was attached to a party from Uppsala who had close contact with a Hammond Watson expedition. The two who worked actually with your grand-father did not last long.'

'None of them lasted long,' said Rachel, as though to reassure him.

'Both men tried to gain access to your grandfather's private hoard.'

Rachel laughed. 'What a wonderful way to describe it! There was a great mass of uncatalogued material — that was all — both in Holland and at home in Northumberland. None of it was a private hoard. With the exception of a few trinkets and a couple of shields, which were hung up for everyone to see, my grandfather kept nothing for himself. All his finds were made for the benefit of historians of every race. And not just historians — anyone who was genuinely, vitally interested.'

He looked down at her with something in his smile that reminded her of the way he had looked at his parents. She didn't want him to look affectionate and sympathetic in that way. She felt no affection for him, and no sympathy; and she wanted none from him.

He said: 'You're still very fond of your grandfather, aren't you?'

'I'd have thought you'd have noticed that sooner.'

'Erik,' he said, 'was fond of his father. Perhaps in the same way — the same loyalty. Can you not feel some . . . some kindness towards him?'

'Kindness?' Rachel exploded. 'After what he did to me? After what I went through with him? And you haven't told me why — you haven't explained why I was put through that hell.'

'I thought the next step would have been obvious. He could not demand too much risk on the part of the friends he sent into your grandfather's employment. There was only one person who would be prepared to risk everything — and that was himself.'

'Yes,' breathed Rachel. 'Of course. But he could not get to know my grandfather under the name of Ascomann. So he persuaded you — '

'No.' Petersen cut her short. 'I must confess this. He did not persuade me. It was my idea.'

'Yours . . . '

'I am afraid so. We were talking. We had been drinking a lot, while he told me what had happened. And I told him what he must do. It made him laugh. And then he began to listen. I thought it was an amusing idea — a joke.'

'A joke,' echoed Rachel dully.

Unexpectedly he caught hold of her arm. His hand was strong and unyielding. She wanted to tug free, but his grip was insistent. He said:

'I am sorry. Then I did not know.'

'Didn't know what?' she demanded unwillingly.

'That you were real. To me, then, you were just a . . . a figure in a picture. A character in a story that I was making up. You understand? I laughed, and I told Erik Ascomann that he must become Erik Flemming Petersen. For just a short time, you see? He takes my passport and other personal papers. And he enters your grandfather's household — not just as an assistant, who may be thrown out in a few days before he has had a chance of exploring everywhere and finding the Gribedyr armlet, but as your husband.'

'How could you possibly have known that such a crazy scheme would work?'

'We could not know,' said Flemming Petersen. 'But the other attempts had failed to work; this was a possibility that had to be tried. I was mad enough to think of it — and my cousin was mad enough to live it.'

'Mad,' said Rachel, trying again to free herself from his grasp. 'Yes, both of you — mad.'

'I did not know what you were like.'

'What's that got to do with it? How could you have dared to do such a thing to any woman?'

'I have told you. I did not know. To me you were unreal. To Erik you were unreal.'

'I was always that,' she conceded bitterly.

'I thought you would be . . . what is your word? . . . a spinster. An unmarried woman, slaving for your famous grandfather. And you would not fail to marry a handsome Dane like Erik.'

'Which I did,' cried Rachel. 'So your summing-up wasn't so far out, was it? You must be proud of yourself.'

'No. Not proud. Not now that I see what I did.'

His fingers tightened. Rachel was pulled round towards him, and suddenly his mouth was on hers, fierce and strong as his hand. She twisted her head away, and with her free hand struck again and again at his face.

At last he let go. Rachel staggered a few steps away and wiped her mouth; the back of her hand stayed pressed against her lips.

She said: 'How could you possibly . . . how, after what you've just been admitting about your dirty little schemes . . . '

'I did not know than that you were beautiful,' said Flemming Petersen hoarsely. 'Now I know.'

Rachel turned away and began to stumble back in the direction of the house. She heard his feet moving swiftly after her through the grass. She tried to hurry, but she did not know the curves and slight undulations of the land as he did. He caught her up; but he did not try to touch her again. Together they made their way over the ridge, into sight of the house with windows that gave out brightness — one reflecting a smear of chalky orange from the sky, another gleaming with a lamp that had been set on the ledge inside.

The silence was unbearable. And there were still questions unanswered. Rachel said, breathless from her hurried, uneven progress:

'What would have happened if he had found . . . that is, when he failed to find the armlet he was looking for, what would have happened? He didn't love me. He hated me. He humiliated me. I see now that it was because I was Hammond Watson's granddaughter. That must have given him a lot of pleasure. When he had given up the search . . . what was he going to do about me?'

They were approaching the house. Flemming Petersen's steps slowed. He stared up at the house, tranquil against the dark flush of night in the sky. He might have been trying to draw strength — or forgiveness — from it.

'Erik,' he said very quietly, 'was going to leave you. When he found the armlet — as he was sure he would do — he was going to return to Denmark and produce it. He was going to tell the full story — '

'But he'd have been arrested. Don't tell me that it isn't criminal in Denmark to marry under a false name, travel on a false passport, steal other people's property . . . '

'Erik's father was dead. The only thing that mattered to Erik was to bring at least his father's name back to life. We discussed two courses of action once he had found the armlet and brought it safely back to Denmark. The first was for him to write to Hammond Watson, telling him that he had found the armlet and was going to make the discovery public. He would then give your grandfather the chance of avoiding scandal by confirming the authenticity of the armlet and at the same time apologizing for having been so harsh in his treatment of Hans Ascomann's theories in the past.'

'My grandfather would never have been blackmailed like that,' said Rachel.

'Not even to hide the fact that he had wilfully concealed the armlet and denied the possibility of its existence?'

'I don't know what he'd have done,' Rachel confessed; 'but he wouldn't have given way like that.'

'So. That is just what Erik felt. That is why he preferred the other method. He would come back to Denmark and tell the story in every detail — admitting his imposture, admitting that he had stolen the armlet from your grandfather, who had been hiding it all this time . . . and showing the whole world how he had

183

'made fools of the two of you.'

'Yes,' Rachel whispered. 'He would have enjoyed that. To hurt and humiliate . . .'

'Your grandfather' — his voice was no longer low and apologetic — 'hurt and humiliated the Ascomanns. Erik wanted not only to prove that his father had been right: he wanted his revenge on the man who had smashed him.'

'He was your cousin,' she accused him, 'and your friend. You were part of the whole thing.'

'I cannot deny it.'

'You would have been involved with the authorities once the truth came out.'

'No. That was something he refused to contemplate. When he announced his story to the world, he proposed to say that he had stolen my passport and various other papers in order to assume my identity for a space of time. It was not implausible. Indeed, if he had wished to do so he could have done it without my assistance. We were known to be close to each other, and he came to see me so often that he would have had ample opportunity for doing such a thing. I was not planning to go abroad, and it was reasonable that I should not notice that my passport was missing. The moment he gave me the word, I was going to discover the loss and report it. Then I could make application for another. There would have been difficulties — but they could have been surmounted.'

'And afterwards — '

'Afterwards,' said Petersen, 'you would have had no problem in getting a divorce.'

'How kind of you!'

'There would be several possibilities. In Danish law it would not be necessary for you to appear before the court. You could apply for a divorce licence, and if you were living out of the country it could probably be arranged for you to make a deposition in a Danish consulate. It is even possible to arrange for a hearing in the court of whichever country you reside in. In the ordinary way you have to appear with your husband before an arbitrator, but that is only a formality — and it applies only if the party seeking the divorce lives within one hundred kilometres of the appropriate court. I am sure something could have been arranged.'

'It's evident,' said Rachel sourly, 'that almost anything can be arranged in Denmark.'

'In your case, perhaps the marriage could have been annulled because of Erik's false declaration, involving the use of a name not his own. If there were any difficulty over that — if the marriage were regarded as a lawful one in spite of the false name — you could ask for divorce after he had been in prison for two years. He would of course receive a prison sentence for use of the false name and for robbery — and a two-year prison sentence is grounds for divorce in Denmark.'

'I doubt whether he would even have had a sentence. Surely that, too, could have been arranged?'

'It might have been a small one,' Flemming Petersen admitted. 'There would have been many who regarded him as a national hero rather than a criminal. But some token punishment would have been awarded.'

'I see. And supposing — insane as it

may seem — I had refused to take divorce proceedings and insisted that he stay married to me?'

Petersen shrugged. 'There would have been ways round that if he had wished to find them. In this country it is not only the innocent party, as you call it in your land, who can apply for a divorce. Things are more complex then — but not insuperable.'

'So everything was very neat,' said Rachel. 'All very smooth and clever.' She moved slowly on towards the house. 'And I suppose he reported every step of his progress . . . you were so precious, such a fine friend, he wrote you a daily report?'

Flemming Petersen's voice was almost inaudible. 'I have to admit that he . . . kept me in touch. I knew what happened — what things he said to you, and — '

'And the sadistic pleasure he got out of humiliating me.'

'He told me too much. I was uneasy at the time. Now I do not know what to say. At Stevinstad it was easy for me to recall things — to prove who I was. Or who I was supposed to be.'

They reached the house and he led the way indoors. The room in which she had sat before was bathed now in mellow lamplight. It drew her welcomingly into its cosy warmth. It was an atmosphere that could make you drowsy; but she was not going to let herself grow drowsy.

Fru Petersen got up from her chair as the two of them entered the room. She spoke agitatedly to her son, who smiled and nodded and answered soothingly. The old woman glanced at Rachel, attempting a smile, and then went out.

'Please sit down,' said Flemming Petersen. 'My mother will not be long. She is preparing a meal — '

'I don't wish to stay for a meal,' said Rachel. If it sounded brusque and ungracious, she did not regret it in the least. 'When we've finished this discussion, I want to go to a hotel — there's a hotel down by the harbour, I imagine?'

'It's not a very good one. In fact, I do not think you would wish to stay there. Our only good hotel is on the other side of the island. You will stay here tonight.'

'Thank you, no.'

'My mother will be most disturbed if you do not stay.'

'You'll have to explain to her,' snapped Rachel. 'You have such a talent for thinking up plausible stories, I'm sure you'll be able to satisfy her.'

Flemming Petersen went and stood by the window. The golden globe around the lamp flame cast a searching light up his face, shadowing his eyes and sharpening the edge of his profile against the dark window.

He said: 'I have told you that I am sorry. I have told you also the full story.'

'Not quite,' said Rachel.

He moved back into the room, towards her. She had a flicker of panic. If he tried to kiss her again she would kill him. Somehow she would bring him down. After what she had suffered because of him, because of his preposterous sense of humour . . .

Desperately she cried: 'You haven't explained why you came to Stevinstad! Why did you pretend to be my husband? How did you come to be there?'

189

'Ah yes,' he said solemnly.

There was a sudden thunderous hammering on the front door. It resounded through the house. Rachel's hands tightened convulsively on the arms of her chair. Her heart seemed to flutter, leap, and fall again.

Petersen went out of the room. There was a murmur of voices along the stone-flagged passage, and then he came back, followed by a man in what was obviously police uniform.

Petersen said: 'This is Olsen, from the village. He has had a telephone call. We have no phone here, there is no way of reaching us. He has brought a message up for you.'

Rachel looked enquiringly at the policeman. He bowed, and returned her gaze, but when he spoke it was in Danish, and he clearly expected Petersen to translate as he went along.

'Mrs Watson has made a call from Stevinstad. She tried to reach you in Copenhagen this morning, but you had gone. It has taken her some time to find out how she could get in touch with you here.'

'Yes, yes,' said Rachel impatiently. She felt apprehensive. Some indefinable threat moved closer to her.

The policeman went on, and Petersen translated, the two voices mingling and blundering over one another.

'The house in Stevinstad was broken into last night. Your grandmother was tied up while thieves . . . went right through . . . opening everything. There is great confusion, she says. You must come back and not go straight on to England. The policeman says' — the policeman was now sounding very awed — 'that Mrs Watson was very angry. He says that he could feel it at this end of the telephone.'

Rachel could imagine that. Her grandmother's indignation at being tied up while the house was ransacked . . .

She said: 'But why was my grandmother the one to telephone?'

'Perhaps because she speaks Danish.'

'Of course. And what about Adrian — Mr Brent? What did she say about him?'

Flemming Petersen's expression was blurred by the shadows cast by the lamp.

In an even tone he asked: 'This Mr Brent means a lot to you?'

'I want to know if he's all right. It *is* because Grandma speaks Danish that she made the call, and not . . . not . . . ?'

Petersen rapped out a couple of questions. The policeman answered them briskly, then added something as an obvious afterthought.

Petersen said: 'He remembers her saying that two of them were tied up. There was nothing about anyone coming to any harm.'

The policeman began to speak again. The story was not finished.

'There has also been a telephone message from England during the day. From . . . a place whose name he cannot speak. He did not catch it.'

'Thingthwaite — in Northumberland?'

The policeman nodded vigorously. *'Jo — ganske rigtigt!'*

Rachel gasped. 'Don't tell me — '

'That, too, has been robbed. Your caretaker there was knocked out and tied up, and the place was searched. The parcels were opened, your grandmother says — things torn, cupboards emptied.'

There was silence. That was all. And enough, too, thought Rachel, dazed.

While she was trying to sort out the implications, Flemming Petersen talked affably to the policeman. After a moment he went to an old wall cupboard whose door creaked protestingly as he opened it. He took out a bottle of aqvavit and three glasses. When he glanced towards Rachel she shook her head abstractedly. The spirit was too potent for her — but not as potent and dizzying as the insistent thought that came clamouring up into her mind.

'*Skaal*,' said Petersen and the policeman; and they drank.

The policeman then clicked his heels and bowed to Rachel. She tried, vaguely, to thank him. But she was not really able to speak until he had gone and Flemming Petersen had come back into the room. Then she said:

'Erik is still alive!'

'No.' He looked staggered, but not by what she had just said. He looked more as though the thought had also found its way into his mind, and he was only now starting to grapple with it. 'It's not possible.'

'Isn't it?' Rachel snapped at him. 'Erik's alive — and you know it. You've been in it together right from the beginning — and you haven't reached the end yet, have you? Spying, prowling around the house . . . and then yesterday, when I was on my way from Stevinstad, the theft of Mr Kennedy's car . . . '

Petersen blinked. 'Theft? What is this about a car and a theft?'

'And now,' she raged on, 'when I am out of the way, the house is ransacked. And our home at Thingthwaite. You must be getting desperate. And now that you've found nothing — because there's nothing to find — what madness are you going to get up to next?'

'I swear to you — '

'He's still alive,' Rachel persisted. 'And how did he manage that? I think' — she threw the words defiantly at him, having gone so far now that her fury was greater than any fear could possibly be — 'Erik murdered my grandfather.'

He shook his head mutely. He looked winded, as though she had kicked him in the stomach.

'And you still haven't told me,' she said, 'why you came to Stevinstad. How did that fit in with your scheme?'

Very subdued, he said: 'When your grandfather died, there were of course many obituary articles in the Danish papers. He was famous in our country. And naturally there was mention of the young man who had died with him. Erik Flemming Petersen, the papers said. That was all. It was Watson who counted, not his young assistant. Some of my friends wrote to me or enquired about me — and I said that it was obviously another Erik Flemming Petersen. In a country where so many are called Petersen or Olsen or Jensen, it is not a matter for surprise. Only I knew who the man was who had died.'

'*If* he died.'

'I obtained a new passport, after some trouble. When you wrote to my parents, I promised that I would reply: I said it was a mistake, and since I was there in front of them, alive, they were ready to believe that it was indeed a mistake! But of course I did not write to you. Then I saw that the monument was to be unveiled. And as I had business in Rotterdam — '

'As a soil chemist?' said Rachel sceptically.

'Not I. Erik was genuinely a soil chemist. I am in the family business — the canning of fish. It is unromantic, yes? But it is a job, as good as any other. We were discussing an alliance with a Dutch firm, and when I visited Rotterdam I decided to come on to Stevinstad. Curiosity took me there — no more than that. But when I saw you with your friend, that man . . . '

'Adrian? Adrian Brent, you mean?'

'He looked very possessive. He was clearly about to take you over. And I thought it would be funny — I am sorry, but at that time it seemed amusing — '

'Your wonderful sense of humour again.'

'I felt I would like to try to finish Erik's job for him. I could not resist the temptation. I wanted to see what would *happen*. That has always been my failing, wanting to see how things will happen.'

'Now you know,' said Rachel. 'Or do you?'

He said: 'I found how real you were. And I was ashamed. And that is the whole story.'

But it was not, Rachel silently protested. In the brief silence that followed, she felt that he had been honest; and yet he could not have told her everything, for there was still no explanation of the theft of Kennedy's car, the disappearance of the bracelets and necklace . . .

'Erik is still alive,' she said. 'Even if he didn't murder my grandfather, he may have disappeared because he wanted to go on looking for the armlet.'

'Why did he not come back to you, then? It would have been easier.'

'I don't know. Perhaps because he was scared. If he found it, he couldn't have publicized it as he would have wished. He would have been suspected of murder.'

'Nothing could have been proved. It is unlike Erik to have been afraid. And it would not have helped. Sooner or later he must show himself. He could achieve nothing by going into hiding.'

Her head was reeling. The complexities climbed over one another like a confused tangle of snakes, writhing and interweaving.

She was conscious of a feeling of nausea. It was caused not only by the dizzy intricacies of the mystery itself: there was also a growing distaste for the unforgotten wrangles in which her grandfather and Hans Ascomann had been involved. Her image of her grandfather was tarnished. His hold on her, she realized, was beginning to slacken. She was horrified by this growing disloyalty; and yet at the same time she was strangely glad. Dead as he was, she had still been living under his shadow. It was time she came out into the light. But the shadow would not lift entirely until she had solved the problems he had left behind him.

Abruptly there was another knock at the door along the passage.

'Olsen again,' said Flemming Petersen. 'He has forgotten part of the message.'

He went out.

Rachel pushed herself to her feet. If Erik were still alive, still fanatically obsessed with his notions about her grandfather . . .

There were footsteps along the passage. Then in the doorway, with Flemming Petersen behind him, was the American, Julius Kennedy. The two of them came into the room.

Kennedy said: 'Now that that cop has beat it, maybe we can have a friendly talk.'

9

Flemming nodded curtly towards a chair.

Kennedy smiled and shook his head. The smile was thin and impatient.

'I prefer to dish it out this way,' he said. 'But don't let me keep you folk on your feet.'

Rachel sank back into her chair. Flemming remained standing, close to Kennedy. They looked like accomplices; but they were both too tense and wary for that.

Rachel said helplessly: 'Mr Kennedy, if you know anything about what has been going on — '

'Don't give me that,' snapped Kennedy. 'You're the one who knows. If anybody knows, it's you. Let's keep it nice and friendly, huh? We can settle this between us, without anyone on either side holding out on the other.' He looked swiftly from Rachel to Flemming, and back. 'All right: where is it?'

'Where's what?'

'It's got to be here,' said Kennedy. 'We've tried everywhere else. It *must* be here.' He thrust his head forward, his chin jutting aggressively. 'It was passed on to you, wasn't it? Passed on by your husband, before he . . . died.'

Rachel stared up at him. 'What do you know about my husband?' she whispered.

'I know that he got there first. When we saw him that night, he laughed. He saw us digging, and he stood there and laughed. And let me tell you, it wasn't funny. The box was empty, and that wasn't funny.'

'I don't know what you're talking about,' said Rachel.

'No? What a pity. I hoped we could do this nice and friendly, like I said.'

Flemming took a sudden step towards him. Kennedy swung to one side, and now there was a gun in his hand.

'Stay right there,' he said.

Flemming looked at the gun and at Kennedy's face, as though judging the distance.

Kennedy said: 'I mean business. I've wasted too much time. I'm not as patient as I was. I want that necklace, and one of you two knows where it is. Maybe both of you.' His lips were tight. Words were forced out through them like curses. 'That guy Petersen . . . he stood and laughed at us. 'You'll never find what you're looking for there,' he said. Oh, he knew all right. He'd been there. And I reckon you two — '

'How did you find this house?' demanded Flemming.

'This is where Petersen used to live,' said Julius Kennedy. 'We'd tried everywhere else, so we had to come here. And who are you, anyway?' The gun was steady, threatening. 'How did you get mixed up in this: how do you figure in it?'

'I am Erik Flemming Petersen.'

'Don't give me that.'

Flemming went suddenly, wildly, for Kennedy's knees. His body crumpled with incredible swiftness, doubled up and then lunged forward under the gun.

The two men hit the floor, and the gun went skidding away.

Rachel got up and dodged across the room, round the two struggling figures.

Flemming was large and powerful, but Kennedy was an accomplished fighter — and a dirty one. She heard a sudden gasp from Flemming, and saw from the corner of her eye Kennedy getting to his feet. Flemming rolled off and tried to force himself up, pushing his hands down against the floor. Kennedy stamped on his left hand, and Flemming rolled away, panting.

Rachel got to the gun.

'Leave that!' snarled Kennedy.

She picked it up and turned towards him. She did not know how to use the gun, but she clutched it in her hand and pointed it at him. He began to advance slowly on her.

Sobbing, Flemming hoisted himself up to his knees.

'Drop it,' said Kennedy. And then he shouted: 'Wellard.'

He kept coming on. Rachel backed away, edging towards the door.

She said: 'I'll fire.'

'You won't,' he grinned. 'Now go on — drop it, and we'll start talking. We'll start all over again.'

Behind her the door opened. Before she could move away, an arm swept round her and the gun was snatched from her grasp.

'Pretty!' said Kennedy approvingly.

Flemming was on his feet. He glared blackly at the two men — Kennedy and the newcomer, a squat, black-haired man who handled the gun as though he knew how to use it and would enjoy using it.

There were footsteps along the passage. Rachel tensed hopefully. But Kennedy smiled, and when the door opened again and old Hr Petersen came in, it was only to have his arms swiftly pinioned behind him by Kennedy.

'Flemming . . . ' There was a splutter of Danish.

Flemming nodded grimly, but did not reply.

Kennedy said: 'All right.' He let go of Hr Petersen and pushed him roughly forward into the centre of the room. 'Let's make it a party. Let's all contribute something. Mrs Petersen can start. We're playing a game of Hunt the Necklace. All right, then. You tell us where *you* think it is, Mrs Petersen.'

'I still don't know what you're talking about,' said Rachel.

'No?' Kennedy's glance flickered towards his companion. 'Wellard, go get some rope. There's bound to be some in a farmhouse somewhere: they use it all the time.'

The squat man handed over the gun and went out of the room. It took him only a few minutes, then he was back with several lengths of rope.

'Tie them up,' said Kennedy. 'Make a good job of it.'

He stood over them with a gun while Wellard tied them all to their chairs. He carried out his orders efficiently: they were firmly secured when he stood back.

'Now,' said Kennedy, 'we'll search the place. Unless, that is' — he grimaced at Flemming — 'you're prepared to tell us where it is. Save yourselves a lot of trouble. We're not too gentle when we go through a place. If you don't want everything busted up — talk.'

Flemming said: 'There is nothing to tell.'

'All right. If that's the way you want it.'

He turned away towards the door, then stopped.

Rachel, thinking desperately of the damage that might be done to the old people's possessions, cried: 'I swear that we don't know what this is all about. If you'd give us some idea — '

'I don't think you need any idea. Are you ready to give out?'

'We still don't know what it all means,' she said.

Kennedy jerked his head at Wellard. 'Better stuff their mouths so they can't start squawking. We don't want a posse of farmhands busting in.'

Wellard was equally efficient with this job. He rammed handkerchiefs tightly into the mouths of the three of them, and fastened them behind their heads. The material bit viciously into the corners of Rachel's mouth. She could hardly move her head. More than anything, she was enraged by the indignity to old Petersen. He had done nothing to deserve this; he ought never to have been involved.

'Let's go,' said Kennedy.

The two men left the room. Rachel

tried to say something, but all she could produce was a strangled mutter. Old Petersen and his son did not even attempt to speak. She sensed their impotent anger.

There was the soft bump of footsteps overhead. Then came a wrenching, splintering noise. Kennedy and Wellard were quite prepared to break the place apart in their search.

If only she knew what it was they were seeking! . . . No archaeological treasure was worth such methods from such men. The references to a necklace had just been baffling.

There was a heavy crash from overhead, followed by a faint sound in the room that might have been old Petersen wincing.

Rachel tried to twist her wrists free, but Wellard had done too good a job.

Flemming grunted once, as though he too were trying to fight against the rope that lashed him to his chair.

The footsteps above receded. The men were going into another room. The sound of their destructive quest was fainter now.

Rachel was facing the door. When she saw it begin to open slowly, she thought at first that there must be a draught along the passage. Then she was sure she heard the sound of breathing. The door continued to open, slowly and steadily. She did not know what to expect.

Then Fru Petersen's head came round the door. She would have looked comic if she had not been so terrified.

Her eyes widened when she saw the three of them. In a matter of seconds she had run into the room and was unfastening the rope that secured her husband. Her hands trembled, and she had little strength in her fingers, but he was soon freed. Then she turned to Flemming.

The two men got up, rubbing their arms, as the old lady set to work on Rachel.

Then there was the sound of feet coming down the stairs. Kennedy and Wellard were on their way back.

Flemming pushed his father back into his chair and looped the ropes quickly round him. He rammed the handkerchief loosely into his mouth, then sank back

208

into his own chair, pulling the ropes as convincingly as possible about him. His mother hurried into the shadows of the chimney-piece.

Kennedy kicked the door open and strode into the room, the gun nosing greedily from his hand.

'We haven't got all night,' he said. 'Maybe it's quicker if we do the job down here.' He walked right up to Rachel. 'Are you going to talk?'

Fru Petersen had hardly begun to slacken the rope. Rachel could not move. She could make only a muffled sound.

Kennedy reached out and tore the bandage from her mouth.

'You going to tell us where it is?'

'I've already told you, I don't know anything about it.'

He drew his hand back with the gun in it. Rachel closed her eyes, bracing herself, waiting for it to be smashed across her face.

Then Flemming had launched himself from his chair.

Wellard yelled something. Kennedy swore, and the gun went off. Rachel opened her eyes, just as two men lurched against her. She was carried backwards and then turned over on to the floor. Kennedy seemed to reel above her, his face distorted with fury. Then Flemming's fist blotted out the face.

Old Petersen staggered up and tried to swing his chair at Wellard. Wellard dodged, and the chair crashed against the wall behind him. He advanced on the old man.

Kennedy was on his feet, and Flemming was down. The gun lay on the floor close to Flemming's hand. He made a grab for it, and got it just as Kennedy tried to kick him in the side of the head.

Old Petersen hit Wellard, but there was no force behind the blow. Wellard sliced him across the side of the face, snapped his head round, and then chopped him savagely across the neck. Petersen sagged. His wife screamed, and came out of the shadows with her hands raised as though to seize Wellard by the hair.

At the far end of the passage a door crashed open and there was a babble of voices. The sound of the shot had brought the farmhands up to the house.

Kennedy looked wildly around.

'Beat it!' he gasped.

Flemming made a despairing attempt to block the doorway. The two of them shouldered him to one side. There was a shout as they hurled themselves into the group of men who were coming along the passage. The shock of surprise was on their side. They broke through and were out of the building.

Old Petersen groaned a command in Danish. His wife added her voice, shrill and outraged. The men hustled back, out into the open again.

Flemming staggered to Rachel's chair and began to fumble with the knots. When she was free, he helped her up. Her arms burned as the blood flowed freely once more. She clung to Flemming for a moment to regain her balance.

'You will stay here,' said Flemming. 'I will go with the others. Those men cannot escape. It is a small island, and everyone will help. I have the gun: they stand no chance.'

She tried to protest, to keep him beside

her, but he had gone. Then Fru Petersen had an arm round her shoulders and was persuading her to sit down again.

'I'm sorry,' said Rachel, on the verge of tears. 'I'm sorry I came here. You oughtn't to have things like this happening to you.'

The older woman, not understanding a word, patted her arm sympathetically. Her husband leaned against the edge of the chimney-piece for a minute or two, then went to the table beneath the wall cupboard, where the bottle of aqvavit still stood. He filled three glasses and brought two of them across to his wife and Rachel. They drank, tossing it back in one gulp. The spirit stung Rachel's throat and then burst up in warmth from her stomach.

In the distance, outside, they heard a rhythmic throbbing noise. In the stillness of the evening it struck an echo from the walls of one of the farm buildings, and then faded away.

Five minutes later Flemming was back. 'They had a boat,' he said tersely. 'A boat of their own. Olsen will send a message along the coast, but it will be time before a patrol can look for them. And it looks like a fast boat. I fear we have lost them.'

His father filled another glass and held it out to him. Flemming drank, and looked into Rachel's eyes as he set the glass down.

She said: 'This . . . all this that has just happened . . . it meant nothing to you?'

'Nothing,' he said. Then he added: 'You believe me?'

'I suppose I must. None of it makes any sense at all. I don't know where to begin — where to start thinking.'

'You know nothing of any necklace?'

She shook her head.

Flemming's parents began to ask questions in Danish. He answered quickly, but judging from their bewildered expressions he was not giving them too many details.

Rachel said: 'I must go back to Stevinstad.'

'I think that would be wise. You must try to find out what all this can mean. Perhaps the secret of it is in your grandfather's papers, or in the many packages you prepared.'

'If so,' she pointed out, 'Kennedy didn't find it. I don't see that I'm likely to be any luckier.'

'You knew your grandfather and his methods,' said Flemming. 'You may see something that Kennedy missed.' He twirled the long stem of the empty glass between his fingers, musing. 'There must be a number of people involved in this. Kennedy and the man Wellard could have gone through the house in Stevinstad and then come here. But they could not also have gone through the one in England. There must be accomplices. And what makes it worth their while to act so?'

'Grandad never possessed anything as valuable as that,' said Rachel.

'Nothing that you know of,' he said meaningly.

Old Petersen shuffled past with his wife on his arm. It did not take any knowledge of Danish to understand that they were going upstairs to assess the extent of the damage that had been done. Rachel was about to make some remark, to ask Flemming somehow to translate her regrets, when he said:

'You will go to Stevinstad, and I will go to Rotterdam. There I have contacts. I will find out what I can about Julius Kennedy — if there is anything to be found.'

'But this is nothing to do with you. It's my affair, really. I think you've been involved too deeply already.'

He nodded grimly. 'That is so. And now I am involved, I will go through to the end.'

'I'd sooner you didn't.' Even to herself, her voice sounded harsh and repellent. 'It would be better if . . . if you had no more to do with me. There's been enough damage already.'

'To you,' he asked softly, 'or to me?'

'To me — and to your parents. I'm not concerned about you.'

'That is a pity. But still I shall go to Rotterdam, and I will tell you what I learn.' He studied her for several intense seconds, so that she longed to look away but would not let herself do so. 'And you,' he said, 'when you get back to Stevinstad, tell your . . . your Mr Brent to take good care of you.'

'He'll do that anyway.'

'He is a weak young man,' said Flemming brusquely. 'I knew it when I first saw him. And I do not make mistakes. He wants only the reflection of your grandfather's fame.'

'You hardly saw him,' Rachel protested.

'Long enough to know that he is not good for you.'

Before she knew what he was doing, he had gripped her shoulders and kissed her.

She struggled, and felt his fingers biting into her. She wanted to cry out, but his mouth was too unrelenting. Then she pushed him madly away. She was bruised and shaken by the kiss. It was an assault, a savage echo of his cousin. And she wanted no echoes of his cousin. She wanted to be back, secure, with Adrian.

10

'But you might have been killed!' said Adrian.

He was pale and very angry. Rachel had finished her story, and as she talked she had watched a baffled fear come and go in his face, followed by this anger. She reached out her hand to him, and he grasped it tightly.

Old Mrs Watson stirred. She looked sour — whether at the clasp of their hands or at the implication of the narrative, it was impossible to say.

At last she muttered: 'We might *all* have been killed.'

The indignity of being trussed up while the house was searched still ached in her bones, a pain as insistent as her arthritis. And probably the thought of the mess there must be at Thingthwaite, the place that was really her home, was even more agonizing.

'I don't think Kennedy was out to kill,'

said Rachel. 'He might have done so in desperation — but if he wants to find what he's looking for, he's hardly likely to murder everyone who might be able to help him.'

'Are you able to help him?' demanded Adrian. 'Do you know something that . . . that you haven't told me?'

She met the challenge of his gaze and forced him to look away. Their hands fell apart. Yet at the same time she was warmed by his concern for her.

She said: 'I still can't begin to imagine what it's all about. On the way back here I tried to fit the pieces into some sort of pattern in my mind. But there's no reasonable explanation.'

'You'd do better to forget about it,' said Adrian. 'Whatever it is, we don't want to be involved in it. The sooner we get back to England, the better.'

Mrs Watson was obviously reluctant to agree with him on anything, but on this point she forced herself to nod. 'I shall be glad to see no more of this country.'

Rachel got up and walked impatiently to the window. She stared out, as though the answer might be somewhere across those grey waves that had rolled up on these shores for so many thousands of years, dragging at the land or adding to it, washing up bodies and wreckage or snatching them out to sea.

'The car theft,' she mused aloud, 'was clearly a fake. Kennedy could hardly have expected to give me a lift that day, but when the opportunity presented itself he grabbed it. When we stopped at the house in Duurwijk he must have gone straight to the telephone and arranged for some accomplice nearby to steal the car. All my luggage was gone through, and a few small items taken. But what could they have wanted with that stuff? It was of no value to anyone except an archaeologist or a historian. Unless . . . ' She watched the white caps of the waves race in towards the dike, and saw the spray leap above the wall. The sky was grey and stormy, and the sea was running higher than she had ever seen it before. It echoed her mood — a mood of frustration, of a furious desire to smash through and open a way. 'There was some mention of a necklace,' she recalled. 'And the things they took from my luggage . . . could the man searching the car have mistaken them for what was wanted, or . . . or might he even have thought they were a cover for the real thing — something concealed inside? But *what were they looking for?*'

'It is of no concern to us,' said Mrs Watson in a surly tone.

'But I want to know. I think it's time we reported the whole thing to the police — '

'Laying what charges?' Adrian broke in. He sounded impatient and fed-up. 'These folk here — you'd have a devil of a job convincing them that there was a strong case for picking up Kennedy. You can't prove the car theft was a fake: he reported it to the police himself, and did everything strictly according to the book.'

'Including holding us up with a gun?' snapped Rachel.

'That was in Denmark. And the ransacking of the house in England must have been done by other accomplices, while Kennedy and his man over here went through *this* place.'

'You know it was Kennedy?'

'We had no chance to see their faces. I was knocked out, and your grandmother was lashed up from behind. But it's fairly safe to assume that Kennedy and the man with him did the job, then pursued you to Denmark.'

'And you still say there's no case for going to the police?'

'We can't prove anything,' Adrian insisted. 'We would need to have the Dutch, Danish and English police working together — and I don't believe they'd start an operation on that scale for what is . . . well, little more than a matter of supposition. The only definite thing that witnesses can testify to is the hold-up at the Petersen home — and even there, if Kennedy denies it all, it'll be difficult to prove anything. It will all take time — a lot of time — and personally I'm in favour of getting home.'

'They might come after us there,' said Rachel. 'Perhaps we'll never get any peace.'

The floor seemed to quiver for a moment under her feet. A huge wave reared up over the dike, and the whole wall trembled. Rachel suddenly became aware of the wind. They were so used to its monotonous howling down the side of the house that she only now began to realize that it had intensified and was rising to a scream.

'Report the details to the police,' said Adrian wearily, 'and we'll have to hang around here for days while they ask questions. We might be hauled back from England at some stage of the proceedings — to and fro, and precious little definite at the end of it.'

'All right,' said Rachel. 'I know there's not much to go on. But perhaps when I hear from Flemming — '

'The Petersen fellow?' Adrian's anger became sharp again.

'He's going to let me know the result of his enquiries in Rotterdam. I'm not going back to England until I've heard from him.'

Something twisted at Adrian's mouth — suspicion, or perhaps jealousy. Again Rachel put out her hand to him, but this time he did not seem to notice. In an odd, detached sort of way she realized that life with him would be difficult: he would be uneasy when she was not with him, querulous, demanding.

Life with him . . . The question had not really arisen yet. The question had not been put.

She had longed to be back with him, getting everything settled and cleared up. But now that she was here, nothing had been settled. Adrian did not want to grapple with the mystery. He was probably right: there were too few clues, and such as there were made no sense. Yet she wanted to go on wrestling with the problem, as she might have wrestled with a crossword puzzle until the final line had been filled in.

If Flemming Petersen could provide just one or two more answers — filling in one line across and one down, so that other answers fell neatly into place . . .

Adrian said: 'If you insist on approaching the police, let's put in a formal report and then leave it to them. We can make it clear that we don't want to be involved in any protracted investigations. We have to go back to England and get on with our own lives, and although we'll answer any queries that are sent on to us, we're not prepared to devote too much time to the business.'

He got up and came to stand beside her. Rachel turned to him, and he smiled. She tried to smile back, but she felt that they were not together: they were hardly even in the same room.

Abruptly she knew what had to be done. She had known all along, really, but had been putting off the conscious admission.

She said: 'Adrian, will you get the car out, please?'

'The car?' He looked meaningly out of the window just as rain slashed great clawing fingers across the glass, blurring the grey tumult of the sea. 'It's a filthy afternoon. What on earth — '

'Please,' said Rachel. 'And I'll go and get a spade.'

She felt quite cool and callous about it, although she was quite sure what they would find.

Adrian still hesitated.

She said: 'If you don't want to come,

I'll drive myself.'

'All right,' he said dubiously. 'But where are we going?'

'I'll tell you the route.'

She went to the side door, letting herself out close to the side door of the museum. The wind almost plucked her from her feet. Funnelled down the passage it snatched at the door and blew it from her hand. She had to put all her weight on the latch in order to close the museum door behind her while she got a spade from the small storeroom.

There was nobody in the museum today. The light from the windows in the roof, carefully pitched to illuminate the main exhibits, was steely and hostile. One end of the main hall was dominated by the battered prow of a Viking long ship carefully reconstructed from a multitude of fragments. Along the walls were glass cases filled with smaller objects — the patient siftings of mud and earth, permanent echoes of a lost world and generations of lost peoples. Rachel, standing in the doorway which led from the storeroom into the hall, was suddenly sure that at any

moment her grandfather would burst
through the door at the far end and
come striding across the floor, raving
about some new stupidity on the part of
the authorities or some pedantic professor from Iceland. She felt him very close
to her again.

The wind buffeted the building, and
she forced herself out of her trance. There
were no ghosts here. Hammond Watson
was gone. This was all that was left of him
— this collection of dead stone, wood and
bronze, these plaster models and dia-
grams.

Some of the cases were standing askew.
The tall cupboards at the end of the room
had been forced open. The intruders had
gone through here just as they had gone
through the house, though they had not
made quite such a mess here: the layout
of the museum was so neat that their
search had been made without the
necessity for such ransacking and over-
turning as there had been in the rooms of
the house.

Rachel glanced down into the nearest
case, set against the wall beside her.

It contained a reconstruction in carefully painted plaster of a typical Viking encampment. This consisted of an outer fort with a rampart and moat, and a main fort also surrounded by rampart and moat. Within the main rampart were barrack huts and the hunched shapes of small houses like upturned ships. The model spoke of a harsh, brutish warrior life that was well over and done with.

Erik, she recalled, had started this model. He had spent a couple of evenings on it, and then he had died and it was left, the wall unfinished and the huts unpainted. Adrian had taken on the responsibility of completing the work. His tidy mind had objected to the ragged edges and half-finished appearance of the model. He had made a good job of it.

And, she thought bitterly, his part of the job had been done during the day, as a duty — not during the evenings as a pleasure. Erik had taken a delight in shutting himself away in the museum and shaping the plaster those evenings — evenings when he should have been with her, his wife, talking to her and beginning to build a life with her instead of building a memorial to dead men; talking, letting her know that he was her husband and that he loved her.

Rachel shook the memory aside and went out into the wind again. She hurried across the narrow passage into the house, found her coat, and went out of the front door to where Adrian was waiting for her in the car.

Along the sea wall the wind was even more ferocious. Spray whipped intermittently across the windscreen, and the car was pushed to the edge of the road. Adrian peered blindly out through the confusion. Rachel would hardly have blamed him if he had turned round at the end of the first half-mile and driven back to the house, refusing to go on. But his mouth was set grimly, as though he had determined to see this through, and he kept doggedly on until at last they reached the foaming tumult of the sluice. Here the road divided, one fork leading on to the old enclosing dam, the other swinging in around the polder and heading inland.

'We turn right,' said Rachel.

Adrian swung the car away from the wind. Now that its force was behind them, they were thrust impetuously away from the sea.

The sky had darkened and the light was uncertain. The features of the land ahead were lost in a threatening twilight. The green of the grass was sombre, and patches of bare earth and mud were almost black. On their right the small enclosed lake controlled by the sluice had risen in a dark fury until it seemed likely to overflow the road.

Adrian said: 'I don't like the look of this. If we can't get back — '

'We'll have to go the long way round.'

'Do you know when high tide is, out there?'

'They've allowed for the highest possible tides,' said Rachel with an assurance she did not feel. 'The wall will stand up to anything the sea can do.'

Adrian wiped the inside of the windscreen with his hand. The wipers flickered before their eyes, tossing droplets and thin streamers of water to either side. The rain began to fall more and more heavily, and the surface of the lake appeared to boil under the assault.

'This is it,' said Rachel. 'Take it on to the side here.'

Adrian slowed, and drove on to the sodden verge of the road.

'The diggings?' he said. 'You can't be expecting to find anything out here? Your grandfather pretty well cleaned this area up.'

Rachel got out, pulling her coat about her. She would be soaked through in a matter of minutes, but that was only an additional incentive to finish the job quickly.

She ought to have put boots on. The mud slopped about her ankles and seeped into her shoes. Adrian got out of the car behind her, then stood there uncertainly. Rachel dragged the spade along, stooping forward to study the surface of the ground as she went.

She knew pretty well every inch of this ground. Her grandfather had spent weeks here, on one of the most fruitful sites that the Netherlands had yet yielded. She had been here on sunny days and in the bleakness of winter, watching while he organized digging operations, and taking notes when he shouted for her. Then Erik had come here with him . . . and since that time she had never been back.

There were mounds of earth where the land had been cleared for investigation. A wide circle had been made round the gravestone which had been found at an early stage. Other holes — square, rectangular, and uneven — marked successful and speculative explorations.

The light was fading rapidly, and it was hard to keep her eyes open against the driving wind and rain. But when she saw the spade marks at one corner of the excavations she was sure that she had found what she was looking for. Nobody else would have noticed the difference in the surface. But she carried a picture of this entire area in her mind — it had been engraven there during those weeks and months of work — and she knew that there was something about this particular corner that was not as it had once been. The difference in the colour of the earth might have been due to the rainfall; but it was not. The faint outline of a rectangle might be a natural feature, or it might be what was left of a brief dig carried out by Hammond Watson and Erik Petersen; but she was sure it was neither.

Adrian was trudging across the slush towards her.

'Rachel, if you're determined to plough around in that mess down there . . . '

He reached for the spade. She evaded him, and stumbled down the brief slope to the main floor of the diggings. Before he could follow, she began to drive the spade into the heavy earth.

'Whatever you're looking for,' he panted, close behind her, 'you can't hope to find anything in this light.'

She lifted a dripping mass of earth and tipped it to one side. It was true that the light was going. But she ought not to have to dig very deep. If what she suspected was true, there would be only a thin layer to get through.

A couple of feet down, the spade struck against something that was soft, but more resilient than the earth. Rachel stopped, and now for the first time she shuddered. Adrian saw it, and again tried to take the spade from her.

'No,' said Rachel. 'This is my job. I'm the one who must . . . who has to . . . '

Gasping with the effort, she dug around the hole she had made, working carefully. She did not want to strike down too forcibly into what lay below. After another ten minutes she said:

'There's a torch in the car, isn't there? I think I could do with it now.'

Adrian went back to the car, and returned with the torch. He flicked it on as he approached, and automatically turned its beam downwards into the hole she had cleared.

Rachel heard the breath hiss drily and painfully in his throat.

He whispered, his words tossed away in the wind: 'Is that . . . is it . . . ?'

'Yes,' said Rachel. 'That's Erik. That's my husband.'

11

They cleared the rest of the earth away from the body with their hands. Once Adrian went away to be sick, and when he came back she could see in the light of the torch that his face was tortured.

She said: 'Go back to the car, Adrian. You don't have to take any part in this.'

'We'll see it through together,' he said. 'But I don't know how you knew . . . I don't know what made you come here.'

'It was Kennedy,' said Rachel, freeing the corpse's right hand from the sticky embrace of the waterlogged earth. 'Kennedy again, up at Hvidfelt. He said something about my husband watching them digging, and laughing, and . . . and there was something about an empty box, too.' She was silent for a few minutes, using all her energy to claw the earth away. Then she said: 'It just began to nag at me — the thought of the two of them in the lake, and Erik perhaps being able to swim away

234

from the sluice and get to land. And where else would he land but close to here — close to the diggings? I don't know whether he killed my grandfather and then swam to safety. If what Flemming Petersen says is true, it doesn't seem to fit in with his plans. He wanted to humiliate Grandad — to show him up, not to murder him. But maybe they had a quarrel — '

'That's something we'll never know now,' said Adrian.

'Perhaps not. But whatever he did . . . whether it was deliberate, or an accident . . . '

Her voice trailed away. The whole of Erik's side was free now, and she could feel something hard in his pocket. She kept her eyes averted from the dead face, and fumbled in the pocket. Adrian muttered something, and rose unsteadily to his feet.

Rachel took out a small object. She knew what it was — the size of it, the feel of it, the texture were all unmistakable.

She said: 'Shine the light over here, Adrian.'

The beam stabbed down, wandered for

a moment, and then found her extended hand. It threw into immediate relief the armlet with the figure of the Gribedyr, the clutching beast within its cage.

'So he found it!' she said softly.

'You mean that's it? Ascomann was right — there really was an original?' Adrian bent over, and the light wavered.

'Keep it steady, please,' said Rachel.

Again the beam fell upon the armlet. She studied it, and then laughed shortly.

'So the old man really did cheat Ascomann!' said Adrian.

She nodded. 'He cheated him. But not by withholding the genuine armlet. I don't believe there ever was a genuine one. This is a fake. You can see it's recent. It's crude and cheap — not nearly as convincing as the one that Ascomann actually found.'

'Then what — '

'I would imagine,' said Rachel flatly, 'that this was a trial run. There was no original, no real armlet. This was just my grandfather's first rough attempt to create a fake. He ought to have destroyed it. Somewhere in the house, Erik must have found it when he was prowling around.'

'So perhaps that day he did lose his temper — '

'And kill Grandad?' Rachel took him up. 'Or at any rate he may have had a violent quarrel and upset the boat. Deliberate or not, the result was the same — Grandad was drowned. And then Erik landed, came over here . . . and found Kennedy and perhaps one of his men, looking for something. And there we are, back at the old question: what were they looking for?'

'If you stay here much longer,' said Adrian, 'your grandfather won't be the only one of the family to die by drowning. Let's get back. We can telephone the police and report what we've found. It looks as though it's inevitable now.'

She sensed that he would have been glad to pretend that this had not happened. He would have preferred Erik to have lain there for ever, undiscovered.

Rachel forced herself to look once more at Erik's head. It was twisted on his shoulders at an impossible angle. The neck had been broken, and from the battered face it was clear that there had been a fight. Perhaps he had fallen, silent before they anticipated it; perhaps the violence of his death had been the result of an outburst of rage on Julius Kennedy's part. Certainly Kennedy had a lot of questions to answer. It was time to get back to Stevinstad and set things in motion.

The rain poured over her and soaked through her clothes. It hammered down mercilessly on Erik's wrecked face. She would have liked to cover him, but there was no sheet or blanket in the car that they could use, and she could not bring herself to shovel earth back over him.

'Coming?' said Adrian.

'Yes.' She took his hand, and he pulled her up. Together they walked back to the car.

They had just reached it when a spurt of flame rose into the sky, etching an orange trail across the livid greyness above the sea. There was an explosion that smacked through the pounding of the wind.

'An alarm rocket!' said Rachel.

'From Stevinstad?'

'It looks like it. It's the right direction. And that means there's danger to the wall.'

There was a new threat now in the surge of wind and rain. Everything was so exposed and defenceless out here. They stood, the two of them, by the car on a flat expanse of land that had once belonged to the sea and could so easily be won back by the sea. The danger that every Dutchman knew was alive and immediate again.

Adrian slid into the driving seat, and Rachel got in beside him. As they bumped back on to the road, two more rockets soared into the air, telling the countryside of the threat to the wall. Telephones would be ringing now; and from houses that possessed no telephone, the warning could be seen in the sky.

Light flickered in the distance on the road along the wall. Cars and lorries were already in movement, taking families from Stevinstad around the polder to the safer land behind. Some took the loop to the south; others came towards Rachel

239

and Adrian and swung inland at the sluice.

One driver leaned out of the window and waved as he passed, shouting something that they could not possibly hear. The sound of his horn drifted back to them, as though he were signalling.

'Probably thinks we're blind, and don't know what's going on,' commented Rachel.

Adrian grunted in reply. He was holding the car against the buffeting of the wind. One could almost believe that the road was shifting beneath the wheels: at any moment great cracks might appear in it, and the boiling cold sea would come rushing triumphantly through.

Another car bounced past them. Rachel glanced back to watch its progress, and saw two headlights in the distance behind them, coming in the same direction.

She said: 'Somebody else is heading back towards Stevinstad.'

'Probably coming to pick up some relatives,' said Adrian. 'They'll be sending in transport from the nearest towns, I imagine.'

'Yes, I suppose so.'

But there was something about those oncoming lights that Rachel did not like. They looked too purposeful. In the sinister, shifting storm-glow, they seemed to be racing after her in deadly pursuit.

'We've got to collect your grandmother,' said Adrian, 'and then get out as fast as we can.'

'All our belongings — '

'There'll be precious little time to get stuff together,' he said. 'I don't think we should allow ourselves more than ten minutes. If the wall breaks anywhere below the road, we'll be cut off.'

A truck coming towards them began to flash its headlights as though signalling.

Rachel said: 'I'm sure he wants to attract our attention. Don't you think we ought to stop, just in case — '

'He only wants us to turn back,' said Adrian. 'We can't afford the time to stop and discuss it with him.'

'You don't suppose one of them has already picked up Grandma? Maybe that's what he's trying to tell us.'

The truck hissed past and was gone.

She looked at Adrian's taut profile, and was alarmed by the grimness of his concentration. He seemed to be unable to think of anything other than the sheer business of holding the car on the road and getting back to Stevinstad as quickly as possible. She must surrender to his determination — which was probably the best thing in the present crisis.

The headlights behind seemed to have fallen away, but they were still there. The cars and trucks from Stevinstad were reduced to a trickle now. Most of them would have taken the opposite direction.

The finger of the monument reeled against the sky, appearing to sway and totter against the turbulent background of black clouds. Stevinstad itself was hunched ahead of them, almost obliterated by the rain.

'Get your grandmother,' said Adrian brusquely as they approached. 'Get her out into the car, while I have a quick check whether there's anything else we can save. And if she's not there' — it was the first indication he had given of even considering the idea that Mrs Watson might already have left — 'grab up anything you want that's ready to hand, and get that out to the car. I'll only be five minutes or so. We mustn't risk any more. I don't want to end my days by drowning in this wretched country.'

He slowed, and turned off the sea road. Rachel shivered. The cold and damp were eating into her. She would have liked nothing better than to go indoors and sit by the fire, listening to the howling of the gale outside and feeling snug and warm . . . Like an Arctic explorer, she thought wryly, sinking down into the snow and letting himself drowse off into that cold yet soothing embrace of death.

As the car stopped she forced herself to move quickly. She got out and went swiftly into the house, her hand reaching instinctively and accurately for the light switch immediately inside the door.

The house was deserted. She could tell at once; she sensed it. One of the trucks had undoubtedly taken the old lady to safety. And she realized in a flash of revelation that for her the house had been emptied not merely of her grandmother's presence but also of the last echoes of her grandfather. Hammond Watson had betrayed his own ideals, and now his grip on her was slackening at last. Flemming Petersen had not been far from the truth. The self-made scholar, setting up his own standards, had not scrupled to forget them when it suited his malicious purpose. The faked Gribedyr armlet had, beyond a shadow of a reasonable doubt, been the work of Hammond Watson. For Rachel, that one piece of treachery undid everything else he had ever achieved.

She walked on into the sitting-room and switched on another light. It was evident that someone — perhaps one of the drivers who had signalled to them along the road — had given her a lift. Rachel felt a reluctant smile plucking at the corners of her mouth. Poor old Grandma! Hardly recovered from the invasion by Kennedy, she had now had to be hustled out of the house and into some car or lorry, to be driven off into the clamorous twilight of the storm.

'Adrian,' she called.

There was no reply. He had not

followed her into the house. Yet he had spoken of seeing what might be salvaged.

Rachel went back to the side door and peered out. There were lights on in the museum.

She clung to the door as the wind shrieked down the passage. She had not suspected Adrian of the fanaticism of a Hammond Watson — or of an Erik Ascomann. And although the loss of material from the museum would be a sad one, there was nothing there of such importance that it would prove irreplaceable.

She darted across the narrow space, letting the door of the house slam behind her, and went into the museum.

The sound of breaking glass met her. That sound . . . and the strange, incredible sight of Adrian smashing a huge axe down at one of the exhibits. He had not set out to wreck the glass case itself: he had removed the top, and as he wielded the Viking axe, taken from the wall above, glancing blows struck slivers of glass from the side panels. His main objective was the plaster model inside the case

— the model that he himself had finished off so expertly. As Rachel stood bewildered just within the doorway, she saw the raised wall of the Viking encampment split by the savage blade of the axe. Twice, three times, four times the blade fell as though carrying out a hasty execution; and fragments of the model spattered out from the case. Then Adrian let the haft slide through the fingers of his left hand. With his right hand he reached into the havoc he had caused, and fumbled under the cracked green wall.

The lights blinked as though with astonishment. For a second they went out, then blazed on again. Somewhere the cables were being wrenched by the storm.

Now the light sparkled and struck back from the necklace that Adrian was holding.

Rachel stepped unsteadily forward.

'Adrian, where did you . . . how long have you been . . . '

He turned impatiently towards her and thrust the necklace at her. 'Hold this. I won't be a minute.' His hands were trembling. The axe swayed. The fingers of his right hand probed through the shattered plaster and brought out two pendants.

'You must have known all along,' breathed Rachel. 'You knew what Kennedy was after.'

'He didn't get what he was after, though, did he?' Adrian shovelled a handful of glistening jewellery into his pocket. 'He didn't get any of it — and the sea's not going to have it, either.'

'But how did you find all this?' she demanded.

Julius Kennedy said: 'That's what I'd like to know, too.'

They turned away from the smashed case and looked down the main hall. Kennedy was standing in the main entrance, with Wellard behind him. The wind slashed coldly along the floor, and the two men came further into the room, letting the door close behind them.

Kennedy's gun came ahead of him, jutting out as he paced across the resonant planks.

'We don't want to waste too much time,' he said. 'Just hand that stuff over — every last little bit of it — and we can get moving.'

His eyes were focused on the necklace that dangled from Rachel's fingers, but the gun was steady and purposeful.

Adrian Brent said: 'This doesn't belong to you.'

'No? Then maybe you can tell me who it does belong to? And maybe you'll tell me why, if it's someone else's property, you've been disposing of the smaller pieces one at a time, in London and Amsterdam?'

Rachel looked at Adrian, marvelling, and found that he had become a stranger. This was an Adrian whose existence she had never suspected. His face had fallen into a sullen slackness, but his eyes were wild and unsettled. She felt that he was on the verge of screaming: she could almost hear the frustrated, animal howl of rage he would make.

'Adrian,' she said carefully, 'I don't understand. What have you been doing here? Adrian . . . '

'It all fits,' said Kennedy. He stopped a few feet away. 'Sorry we've made life a bit rough for you, lady. I reckon you genuinely didn't know what was going on — unless,' he added dourly, 'this is all part of the act. You were sure in a mighty hurry to get back here from Hennesø. Guess this is where it's been kept all along.' The gun still pointed ominously at Adrian. 'All right. For the last time. Hand that stuff over. It must have struck you as a pretty set-up, huh? How did you find it? The way I see it, that Petersen guy dug it up from where we stashed it years ago, and when you moved in you found it while you were doing your own snooping about. Right?'

Adrian made no reply. But none was needed. That much of the truth, at any rate, was clear. Erik had come across this hoard during those couple of days on the diggings with Hammond Watson, and had removed it all to the house. Had he intended to keep it, or had he put it away for the time being as a possible pawn in his perverse game with her grandfather? Death had intervened before he could make any use of it. And Adrian had somehow found the things — the necklace, the bracelets, the pendants and whatever those other gleaming treasures were that he had dropped into his pocket;

he had found them and skilfully concealed them in the wall of the model encampment, presumably until such time as he could dispose of them.

'Wellard,' rapped Kennedy, 'go and get that stuff off him. And if you make trouble, brother, you'll get a bullet in you. I've waited too long for this little collection — I'm liable to get sore if anything else happens.'

Rachel said: 'You murdered my husband.'

The American's pale eyes narrowed. 'You don't want to go around saying things like that, ma'am.'

'He came across you digging for these things,' she said stubbornly, 'and because he laughed at you, you set on him and killed him.'

Kennedy said: 'There was an accident.' His voice was as pale as his eyes. 'It wasn't the way we wanted it. He just got too rough, and wouldn't answer our questions. Believe me, that wasn't the way we wanted it to go at all.'

'But it did,' she said. 'It did, and you killed him.'

'You know too much,' said Kennedy, 'or you're guessing too much. Either way, I'd advise you to take it easy. We aim to take what belongs to us and get out of here — and if you play it our way, there needn't be any further trouble.'

Adrian spat words out between his teeth. 'You won't get away with this. Theft is one thing — murder's quite another. You'd do better to clear out and forget about your little haul. It doesn't belong to you any longer. I'm not going to hand any of it over to you — and you're not going to risk putting a bullet into me. So get out. Now.'

'You're crazy,' said Kennedy. 'Wellard — go on, like I said. Dig it out of him.'

Wellard stepped forward.

The lights dipped again, flickering down into near darkness and then coming on full once more. There was a sudden bang from the fuse-box above the storeroom, and the lights all along one wall went out abruptly.

The change of light cast a flurry of shadows across the group near the shattered case. Kennedy edged a pace backwards. At the same time Adrian, with a frenzied, desperate laugh, swung the huge axe above his head and slammed it down again.

Kennedy yelled once. His gun went off, but the bullet ripped into the wall, high up near the ceiling. Then the axe blade split through his head. He lurched forward. The weight of his sagging body, taking the axe down with it, pulled the haft from Adrian's grasp. Kennedy went down, the blood pumping over his shoulders and beginning to make a new, darker shadow across the floor.

Adrian stooped quickly and picked up the gun. When he stood up, he reached with his free hand for Rachel's arm and gripped it tightly. He turned the gun towards Wellard, who was cowering away from the crumpled body and paid no attention as they edged past him.

'Now,' Adrian said, 'we're ready to leave.'

12

Now it was not only the wind that flung the car from side to side of the road. Adrian was driving like a madman, relying on some angel or devil to look after him. The wheel fought beneath his hands. Once his foot slipped right off the accelerator, and the car yawed wildly.

Adrian laughed.

Rachel choked back the sobs of panic that were rising in her throat. She tried to speak above the howling of the wind and yet keep her voice steady.

'Adrian . . . we can't go on.'

'You think we're going to stay there and wait for the waves — or the police?'

'What's happened to you?'

'What's happened?' he shouted jubilantly. 'I've got my hands on a fortune — that's what's happened. And all thanks to your poor dead husband. Ironical, isn't it? But there's some justice in it: you must admit that. Not only do I get you back from him, but I get a dowry as well, as it were.'

Still she tried to sound calm. 'What are all those things you put in the back — those things, and this?' She was still incredulously holding the necklace.

'You certainly didn't check through the house properly after your husband had gone, did you?' The car slowed as Adrian turned to look at her, grinning with delight at his own cleverness. 'I hadn't been in the place a week before I found them, tucked away at the back of the drawer in the desk you told me he used. He couldn't have had time to hide them properly before he died.'

'Perhaps,' said Rachel contemptuously, 'he had no intention of hiding them.' If Flemming Petersen's story had been true, then she owed her husband at least this — the admission that he might have been a fanatic about his father's memory and reputation, but was unlikely to be a thief. 'He might have intended to report them to the authorities — '

'That's a likely one! I suppose you'll be telling me next that he told your grandfather all about them as well?'

'Not necessarily. He hated my grandfather. He may well have kept the discovery from him. He may even have had some complicated idea of using the things in his own warped scheme. But that's not the point now. They're dead, both of them. And Julius Kennedy is dead. And what you're doing is stealing — '

'From Kennedy? Or from your husband?'

'From whoever the original owners were.'

'You don't have to worry about them. No need to get soft-hearted. They were Germans — good Nazis, too. The Schaumburg-Lippe family.'

Abruptly he stamped on the brake. The car slithered over the road, then came to a standstill on the inner edge, looking down into the dark polder. Adrian reached for the necklace and took it from Rachel's fingers. Before she realized what his intentions were, he had unfastened the clasp and slipped the necklace round her neck.

'Adrian, no . . . '

'There,' he said. 'There.' He might have been asking her to thank him for providing her with such a wonderful present, bought specially for her. 'Doesn't it make you feel . . . can't you actually *feel*, from the touch of it, how rich we're going to be?'

'You must be mad.'

Adrian shook his head. 'No, not mad, my dear. Just sensible enough to know that we can lead a much more comfortable life with a certain — ah — capital than if I had to slave away at my job, kow-towing to a lot of old dodderers, putting up with insults from men like your grandfather — '

'Putting up with them,' said Rachel bitterly, thinking how right the old man's judgment of Adrian had been, 'in order to hang on to their coat-tails and scrounge your way through life.'

'At least I won't need to do that now,' said Adrian blandly. He could not take his eyes off the necklace, gleaming faintly in the interior of the car. 'This should make up for the way the family let me down. Never had enough money — just enough to give me ideas, but never enough to fulfil them. A man of my education, a mere slave to fools and weaklings . . . ' He put the car into gear again, and they began to move slowly forward. 'I've been disposing of bits here and there — that's what put Kennedy on the track — but I want to be sure of my contacts before I unload the big stuff.'

'You'll never get it out of the country.'

'I haven't done too badly so far, considering it's not my profession!' He laughed. 'Anyway, I can get rid of a lot in Amsterdam if I have to — though I don't trust these Dutchmen.'

Ahead, blurred by the rain, two distant headlights sparkled like the reflection of some light from inside the car. Adrian did not seen to notice them. His head turned again towards Rachel, nodding convulsively with self-satisfaction.

'You'll soon get used to the idea,' he said. 'I can tell you, we're going to have a very comfortable time from now on.'

A picture seemed to swim across the windscreen before Rachel's eyes — a picture of the model encampment which

Adrian had so cunningly constructed as a perfect hiding-place for his haul, and below it the huddle of a man on the floor.

She said: 'When the police come to Stevinstad and find Kennedy — '

'They won't know we had anything to do with it.'

'That man with him — Wellard . . . '

'True,' said Adrian. But there was no real concern in his voice. The car picked up speed. 'It was self-defence: you'll back me up on that. And we can deny any knowledge of jewels. They couldn't prove anything. They — '

'Look out!' she cried.

The approaching headlights were suddenly huge and dazzling, splashed and distorted by the rain. Adrian twisted at the wheel, trying to pull himself back to his own side of the road. The car skidded, and the lights blazed for a moment, then swept past. Adrian pulled again, this time twisting the car right across the road again. The whole earth seemed to be moving: there was nothing solid, no secure surface.

Rachel screamed.

There was a sudden emptiness beneath them. The car drove off the road and over the edge of the wall, plunging towards the bed of the polder.

It struck. Rachel was thrown forward. Her head smacked against the windscreen, and she felt as though she had been caught up in a whirlpool. The darkness dissolved into colour, and the whole world made a dizzy dance before her.

But they were still upright. Rachel shook her head, and groped uncertainly for the door handle.

Beside her, Adrian moaned but did not move.

She ought to have turned towards him, but the stiffness of the door handle aroused a sudden panic in her. She shook it wildly. The door was twisted, and she realized that her lap was full of slivers of glass. Frantically she heaved against the door, and it gave way. She tumbled out into the rain.

There was very little wind down here, in the shelter of the wall. It howled above, on its way across the polder.

Her knees were weak. She wanted to

collapse. The misery of the cold and rain struck down at her, and the thought of Adrian crumpled in that car gave her a convulsion of fear. The fear had been growing within her since they left the museum; and now that she was standing away from him, out in the open, she could let it take possession.

She looked up despairingly, just at the moment that a torch beam stabbed down from the wall.

'Are you all right?'

It was Flemming Petersen.

She was sobbing as he groped his way cautiously down towards her. When at last he floundered across the boggy, sodden ground, she let him put his arms round her, and sagged against him.

'Come along,' he said gently. 'You must get indoors. It is not safe here.'

She gestured helplessly towards the car. She could not speak.

Flemming took a couple of steps away from her and probed into the inside of the car with the torch beam. In its searching light the face of Adrian came slowly up from the wheel, turning towards them, his eyes narrowing against the brightness.

'I'd better give him a hand. Here — hold this.' Flemming passed the torch to Rachel, and stooped inside the car. She heard Adrian groan, then Flemming was backing away, helping him out.

Adrian stood upright, swaying. He muttered something to himself, but it was inaudible. Flemming tried to urge him towards the foot of the wall. Adrian lurched away from the car, then stopped dead.

'Get the stuff,' he mumbled. 'Got to get it . . .'

'Come along,' Flemming rapped.

Rachel moved to Adrian's other side and began to help him in the scramble up the grassy inside of the wall. As they reached the top the wind caught at them again in its full fury, and they were almost blown backwards.

The lights of a car were visible thirty or forty yards away, the headlights facing towards Stevinstad.

'Your car?' asked Rachel.

'Hired,' said Flemming. 'I came to find you, to tell you about Kennedy. But I did not expect to have to rescue you like this!'

They were still holding Adrian's arms and helping him along. He seemed to become abruptly aware of this. Without warning he twisted free and staggered back towards the edge of the wall.

'Don't go down there!' yelled Flemming. 'Wait until it is daylight. It will be safe then. Now it is not safe. The wall . . . '

The wind threw the rest of his words away. And beneath their feet the ground shifted uneasily. In spite of the darkness, Rachel found that she could see; her eyes were growing accustomed to the swirling blackness. The road was a lighter thread running away into the storm. The seething flecks of whiteness that seemed to thrash in the air only a few feet away must be the foam on the incoming breakers, attacking the sea wall.

'Adrian!' She added her voice to Flemming's.

But Adrian was gone. In the torch's beam they saw him stumbling down the grass towards his car.

Then Flemming caught Rachel's arm.

'The dike — it is going!'

The road seemed to rear up and then crack, two hundred yards away . . . between them and dry land. A new full-throated voice was added to that of the wind. The water raced in triumphantly, throwing all its forces into the opening breach.

For a moment that was a lifetime, there was a tense, quivering balance. Then the wall dissolved and fell back upon the floor of the polder. The sea smashed in, and bored down on Adrian Brent in a vast, clamorous wave.

It was all over so quickly that one could almost have believed there had never been a man and a car down there. In a second the two shapes had been swallowed up and made a part of the devouring water. Spray flew up above road level. The waves jostled through the breach, and then, after the exuberance of that first attack, began to smooth out. Tomorrow there would be a huge lake here — a placid lake, once the tide and the wind had fallen, a blandly innocent surface that would deny all responsibility for the body that was now being carried away, battered along until it reached the shallows where it could lie at peace.

'Nothing we can do,' said Flemming.

He hurried her towards the car.

'But we can't get away now.' The realization that there was an impassable gulf between them and the safe land beyond the polder gripped her throat.

'We will go to Stevinstad.'

'But if the dike breaks all the way along — '

'It is unlikely. And there is not much more tide. I think the houses will stand safely enough. And there is nothing else we can do.'

They drove back along the road which she had so recently travelled with Adrian. Was it her imagination that told her the wind was slackening: was the storm really losing its force, or was it just that she felt safer with Flemming Petersen than she had felt with Adrian?

Safer than with anyone else she had ever known.

She stole a glance at him. He was staring straight ahead at the road, as though daring it to crack up in front of him. His lips were tight.

When he became aware of her eyes on him, he said: 'What had Brent in that car that was so precious to him?'

'Jewels,' said Rachel.

Her hand went up to her throat. She touched the necklace. Flemming slowed the car, and turned to look at her.

'Where did that come from?'

'It's one of the things he stole. Or, rather, that he found. After Erik — your cousin — had found them, that is.'

'When we get back to Stevinstad,' he smiled, 'you must tell me the full story. In the right order.'

'He said something about a German family,' she said. 'The . . . what was it? . . . Schaumburg-Lippe royal jewels. Something like that, anyway.'

She heard his faint whistle, although his mouth hardly appeared to move. Then he said: 'So that was it.'

'You know about them?'

'I remember the case. And it fits in with what I was told about Kennedy by my friends in Rotterdam. Or, rather, what they half-remembered and half-guessed.' He rubbed the inside of the windscreen with his hand, and peered ahead. 'Kennedy was in the American army — in Intelligence. He interrogated some pretty important people when the Allies began to take over Germany. And that may have been when he heard of the jewels. Or maybe he came across them by accident, as with the Hesse-Darmstadt jewels. Those were worth a fortune. Some Americans discovered them hidden in a cellar, and quietly removed them. The family did not know what had happened, and by the time they discovered that the jewels were not in official keeping it was difficult to track the culprits down. Here, also, I think there may have been such a case. At the time of the theft, there were only three aged members of the Schaumburg-Lippe dynasty left — an old man and two decrepit sisters. I remember the newspaper reports a year or two after the war. Only one of the sisters survived then, and she claimed that the family heirlooms had been stolen by the occupying powers. Nobody ever found out quite what had happened — and as the woman was so old, and very strange in the mind by that time, it was difficult to carry out a proper investigation. Now we know what happened. Kennedy found the jewels, and hid them away here in Holland. I do not know why — '

'He was based in Holland,' Rachel remembered. 'He said something about it to me when he gave me the lift that day. But why didn't he get the stuff out of the country when the war was over?'

'It seems strange,' Flemming agreed. 'It may have been that there were strict searches, or he went back unexpectedly, or — '

'But of course!' she cried. 'I know why.'

'So?'

'He buried the jewels near here, close to what was probably his headquarters then. And,' she said slowly, 'he chose a spot which was inundated through a break in the dike shortly afterwards. The entire area was flooded. It was some years after the war before reclamation work could start on that area, and by then he had doubtless been sent back to America and was out of the army. Perhaps he came and prowled around here year after year, desperately trying to think of some way of getting at his haul. Perhaps, even when the water had been drained, the configurations of the land had been smoothed out so much that he couldn't find the original site. He had to take other men into his confidence in an attempt to find out where the jewels were — or maybe they were in with him from the beginning.'

Flemming nodded. 'This is, in essentials, the truth of the story.'

'When they stole those old bracelets and the necklace, it was probably because they thought the jewels were concealed inside the crude, heavy workmanship of the older things.'

'Such detailed questions,' said Flemming, 'can be answered by Mr Kennedy — if we ever see him again.'

Rachel shuddered. 'Kennedy will never answer any questions again.'

'You mean — he is dead?'

'Adrian killed him. He must still be there . . . in the museum.'

Stevinstad appeared before them, shouldering its way up out of the rain. Water streamed across the road, but the place looked secure enough.

Flemming turned towards the side road. The water spurted up from beneath his wheels.

There were no lights on anywhere in the small cluster of buildings. It was an abandoned town, offered back to the sea. But the offer had been rejected. The sea no longer had the strength that had driven it on until this moment. The aggressiveness was draining away, and the voice of the storm was softer.

Rachel got out of the car and hurried into the house. She tried the light switch just to be sure, but was not surprised when nothing happened.

Flemming, behind her, said: 'There are lamps or candles, perhaps?'

'I know we've got a lamp somewhere. In the cupboard, if I can grope my way across to it.'

She bumped into a chair, but found the cupboard. The small oil lamp that stood on the shelf was half-full of paraffin. When Flemming lit it, the flame was the most beautiful she had ever seen: it spoke of light and warmth, and security. Stevinstad was secure.

'I will take the torch,' said Flemming, 'and go to see what you tell me there is in the museum.'

'Don't be long.'

'You will be alone for a few minutes only,' he assured her gravely.

When he had gone, she took the lamp and went through into her grandfather's study. She felt an absurd desire to test herself. Standing in the middle of the room, with the lamp casting elongated shadows along the floor and up the walls, she waited as though for a sign. She had so often seemed to hear his voice in here after he was dead. But now there was utter silence. Yes, she had been right: the knowledge of his weakness had banished him from her mind.

And now there was emptiness. Hammond Watson had finally gone; Adrian Brent had gone. Yet there was nothing frightening in the emptiness. Already she felt that it would soon be filled.

The side door opened and closed, and she heard Flemming coming back. The beam of his torch flickered across the doorway in search of her.

'You . . . you've seen?' she whispered.

'Yes. I have seen.'

'The other man — Wellard?'

'He is not there. I do not think he would have stayed. I think he has gone into the night. He may be walking through the rain. It cannot be enjoyable for him, out there, with the memory of what he has seen. He may have died in the storm. But there is nothing we can do.'

There was a sudden flurry of rain against the window, then it died away. All that was left was the blustering wind — and the sound, strangely remote and ineffectual now, of the surf beating against the wall.

Rachel said: 'I suppose it really is all over now — Erik and his quest, and Kennedy and the jewels, and . . . and Adrian? All over.'

Flemming came across the room. Gently he took the lamp from her and set it down on her grandfather's desk. Then his arms were around her. She let herself cry, but not because she was unhappy: she was tired, and at the same time aware of a terrifying joy that was too sudden to be understood in this one moment, but that would become clearer.

'That part of it,' said Flemming, 'is over. But there is much that is only just beginning.'

He kissed her. His lips tasted salt, like the spray that blew in from the sea.

Rachel tried to protest, to say or do something that would preserve her from this surrender. There were practical things to be thought of; so many things would be crowding in on them.

'So many explanations,' she said, pulling her head away. 'There'll be so much to explain to them — the police, and reporters, and goodness knows what else.'

'Not at once,' said Flemming. 'You will have plenty of time to rest. And when they do come, it will all be easier than you think. They cannot harm you.'

'No,' said Rachel wonderingly, 'I don't think anyone can harm me now.'

He reached for the lamp again and picked it up. With his free arm he guided her across the room.

'You must rest. We will be safe now. The sea has lost another battle in its endless campaign. There will be much damage, and many repairs will be necessary. But Stevinstad will not be threatened again tonight; and in the morning people will come back to see what has happened, and then we will talk.'

'We must talk now,' said Rachel. She realized that she had not yet told him about her discovery of her husband's body. She said: 'While you were in Rotterdam, I . . . I found Erik.'

'Erik?' He stopped, tense.

'Yes. He had been killed. Accidentally, from the way Kennedy was talking, but . . . '

'Perhaps you are right,' he said. 'There are some things which should be said now. I would like to know about Erik — about the end of his quest.'

'I've got a lot to tell you, really.'

His arm tightened across her shoulders. 'I have plenty of time to listen.'

And tomorrow, she thought — or, if not tomorrow, then in a few days' time or a week's or a month's time — they would talk of different things. They had so many things to tell each other, a little at a time; things which would grow in importance until the memory of Erik and her grandfather and Julius Kennedy and Adrian Brent had faded away into the past.

There was no longer any threat in the sound of the wind outside. There was no longer any threat from her past. Now there were only the present and the future.

There was plenty of time.

THE END